The Toby Baxter Book 1:
The River Elf, the Giant, and the Closet

Lighthearted and conspiratorially didactic; an agreeable romp toward adulthood.—**Kirkus Reviews**

Readers will love Toby's slightly tongue-in-cheek fantasy adventure quest, drawing as it does on a wealth of popular culture snippets, from *King Arthur* and *The Hobbit* to *Diary of a Wimpy Kid* and *Star Wars*. Wright's narrative voice is quirky and engaging but does not obscure the important messages in the narrative about what it means to be heroic. Overall, *Toby Baxter* is an exciting adventure and a thought-provoking exploration of what it means to grow from boy to man.—**The Children's Book Review**

The Adventures of Toby Baxter is a fantasy mystery of epic proportions-and it's captivating from page one. The reach of this book extends from middle- grade readers all the way to adults of any age. Try it, you'll see what we mean. The pages are full of intrigue and twists and mystery-all while Toby struggles to find his place and purpose in his new world. The setting is lush, the creatures are awesome-and just as lovable as the characters, and the bad guys are pretty freaking scary. Full of fun, rich in suspense and brimming with adventure!—**readingwithyourkids.com**

Engrossing and addictive... A page-turning middle-grade fantasy.—**The Prairies Book Review**

The Adventures of Toby Baxter

The River Elf, the Giant, and the Closet

Tim Wright

Book 1 of the Adventures of Toby Baxter
The River Elf, the Giant, and the Closet

Free Stuff!
Sign up here: www.TimWrightbooks.com
For the free Prequel: I.C.E. Call Toby Baxter
And a free PDF for Parents on the power of Adventure Books for kids
And be the first to know when Toby's next adventure is released

Copyright ©Tim Wright, 2022. All rights reserved. No part of this publication may be reproduced, stored, or transmitted in any form or by any means, electronic, mechanical, photocopying, recording, or scanning, or otherwise without written permission from Tim Wright. It is illegal to copy this book, post it to a website, or distribute it by any other means without permission. ISBN 978-1-66784-963-8 ebook 978-1-66784-964-5

To

Clover, Phoenix, Decker, Judah, and Mathilda

Do the right thing. Always.

Find your way forward.

Use your gifts and abilities in the service of others.

Be yourself.

CONTENTS

CHAPTER 1
Toby Baxter Sees Things — 1

CHAPTER 2
"My Pajamas Aren't Waterproof!" — 9

CHAPTER 3
Toby Baxter Turns 13 — 17

CHAPTER 4
Back into the Closet — 27

CHAPTER 5
Toby Baxter Has Lots of Questions — 34

CHAPTER 6
Before the Beginning — 40

CHAPTER 7
The Honorary Footie Elf — 47

CHAPTER 8
Toby Baxter Gets Some Answers—
And Doesn't Like Them Very Much — 55

CHAPTER 9
About that Quest — 63

CHAPTER 10
The Drone — 68

CHAPTER 11
Betrayal — 72

CHAPTER 12
You Wouldn't Happen to Have a Slingshot and Five Stones? — 79

CHAPTER 13
Couldn't We Take a Bus? — 82

CHAPTER 14
Into the Woods — 88

CHAPTER 15
> A Simile, a Metaphor, and a Symbol — 95

CHAPTER 16
> On the Run — 101

CHAPTER 17
> Face to Face with a Troll — 107

CHAPTER 18
> A Costly Miscalculation — 113

CHAPTER 19
> Off to See Clygon — 122

CHAPTER 20
> How Will You Use Your Power? — 130

CHAPTER 21
> Clygon! — 137

CHAPTER 22
> Wait! What Just Happened? — 148

CHAPTER 23
> The Surprise — 160

CHAPTER 24
> Grandma Baxter — 164

EPILOGUE — 168

The Adventures of Toby Baxter Book 2:
RiverHome for the Holidays (Excerpt) — 172

hero

[**heer**-oh]

a person noted for courageous acts or nobility of character

a person who, in the opinion of others, has special achievements, abilities, or personal qualities and is regarded as a role model or ideal

--Dictionary.com

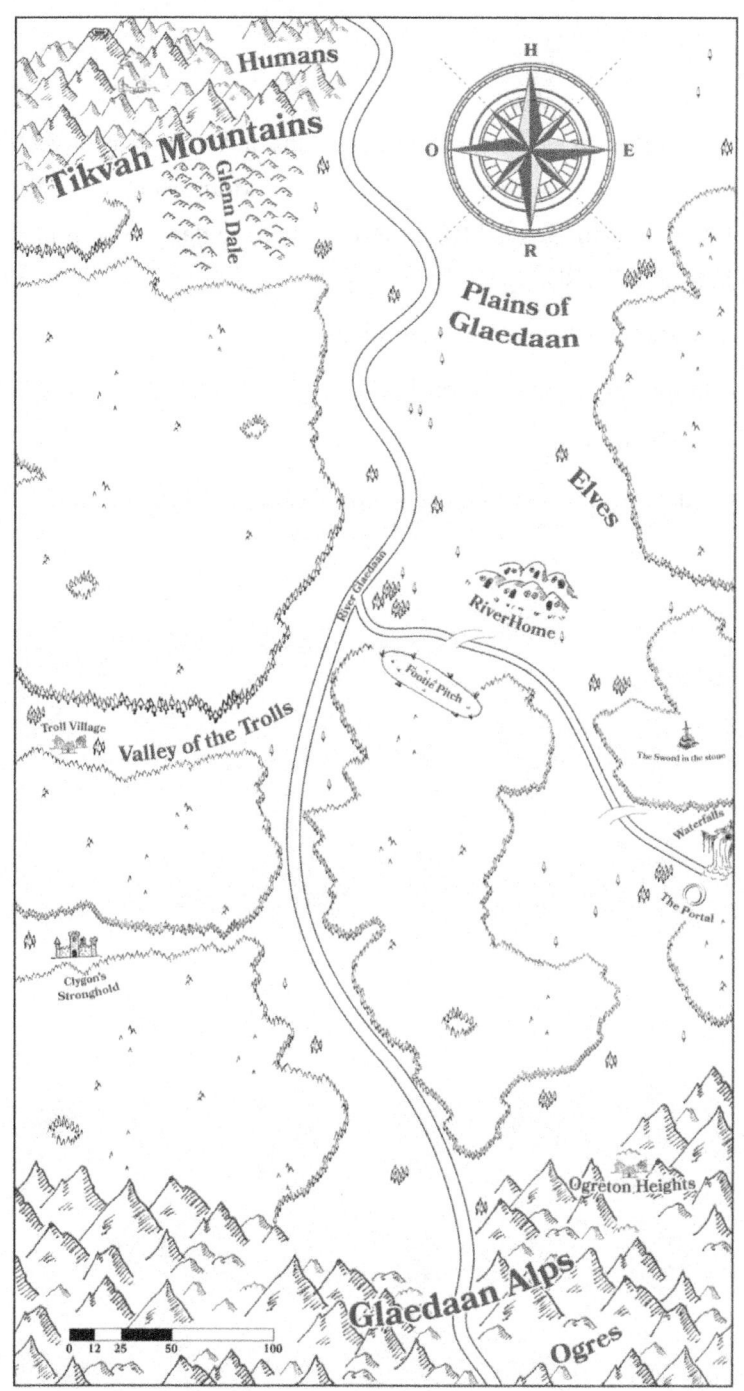

Down the stream toward the water falls, just outside of *RiverHome*, on the side of a hill, stands a sword. *The* Sword. Mounted in stone. Serving as guardian over the River Elves. Alerting them to danger. Summoning a Hero in times of crisis.

For years the Sword has been silent.

But now an enemy approaches.

The Sword begins to glow.

And below the Sword these words: ***I.C.E. Call Toby Baxter***

CHAPTER 1

Toby Baxter Sees Things

The Hobbit. By J.R.R. Tolkien

Toby Baxter opened the book.

He read the first line.

Something about a hobbit living in a hole in the ground.

He sighed.

Then he yawned.

Toby Baxter hated reading books.

It's not that he wasn't a good reader. It's not that he didn't like to read. Unlike many of his friends who spent their free time playing video games, Toby spent much of his free time reading comic books. *Marvel* comic books. His favorite *Marvel Hero* was *The Amazing Spider-Man* with *Captain America* a close second. His room seemingly overflowed with comic books and graphic novels, most of them well worn from being read multiple times.

His friends, though not avid readers, were excited about reading *The Hobbit* as a class assignment. Most of them had read at least some of the *Harry Potter* series and a few of the *Percy Jackson* books.

Toby had tried them, too.

But books take too long to get to the point. Books take too long to read. Comic books start with a bang and don't let up until the end. And you can read them in a few sittings. Books are boring. Why can't comic books count as reading? Take the *Wimpy Kid* books, for example. A book written in the form of a comic book. And funny, too!

Toby closed the book and looked out the window. It was the last hour of the last day of the school week. A good time for daydreaming. A beautiful October fall afternoon. The leaves just starting to turn colors.

Through the second-floor classroom window he could see the acorn trees lining the sidewalk and street just in front of the school. Across the street was the football/soccer field. And beyond the field ran another street with houses built back in the 1950's. Old houses. Older than his grandfather was. Before Grandpa died.

As he stared out the window a movement caught his eye down below. A little boy was running on the sidewalk in front of the school. Nothing unusual about that. But just as Toby was about to look out across the field again the boy stopped—right below Toby. He looked straight up at Toby, his eyes wide with... fear? Intensity?

He was the strangest little boy Toby had ever seen. He appeared to be about four to five feet tall, at least from Toby's vantage point on the second floor. His hair was curly brown. His clothes seemed out of place for a boy so young. They looked like the kind of clothes one might wear in a fantasy novel when headed out on a long quest. The colors appeared to be a mix of forest green and brown with a splash of yellow, perhaps made of leather, although it was hard to tell from that distance. His feet were furry. *Were those really his feet?* His stomach seemed a bit large for a little boy. And his face... it didn't look like a little boy face. It was the face... of a grown man! It was such a freaky sight that Toby almost jumped out of his desk seat. The boy... the man... whatever he was... seemed to be looking over his shoulder and then back at Toby. He was mouthing something. And

Toby immediately knew what he was saying because, making matters even weirder, the man's/boy's words were printed above his head as he spoke, almost like in a comic book:

Toby Baxter! It's your time! We need you!

"Toby!... Toby!... Toby Baxter!" A hand touched his shoulder and this time he did jump. He looked up at his teacher, Mrs Grayson.

"Toby, you seemed miles away."

Toby looked up at Mrs Grayson, trying to get his bearings. He looked back out the window but the boy—the man—was gone.

Mrs Grayson leaned over and whispered almost conspiratorially: "Were you thinking about your big birthday party tomorrow?"

Mrs Grayson was not only his English literature teacher. She was also his mom's best friend. She always knew too much about Toby and his mom knew too much about how he was doing in English Lit. Not very convenient.

Toby was turning thirteen on Saturday. He was having a big *Marvel*-themed costume party. He would be dressing up as *The Amazing Spider-Man*. Because he was turning thirteen, he could invite twelve friends to the party. So far he knew *Thor, Black Panther, Captain Marvel,* and *Black Widow* would be there. And *Batman*. His dad insisted on dressing up as *Batman*. The *Batman* from some ancient 1960's TV show that Grandpa Baxter used to watch when he was a kid, and apparently Dad watched in re-runs. Whatever! He didn't know what the rest of his friends would choose as their heroes.

"Even though it's your birthday tomorrow, remember to read the first three chapters of *The Hobbit* by Monday! Happy Birthday."

Toby picked up his copy of *The Hobbit* and paged through to the end of chapter three. Sixty-three pages! Sigh!

Then the bell rang. School was finally over.

Toby stuffed *The Hobbit* into his backpack and ran down the hall, through the doors, and raced toward his bike. He threw on his helmet, climbed onto the bike, and headed north. He rode past the big park with the huge round water tower in the middle of it. He carefully looked both ways as he crossed one street, and then another, before he rode the short, gradual block-long incline to his house.

His house was built on a slight hill near the end of a cul-de-sac, perfect for playing baseball. The "ground floor" of the house sat on the top of the small hill. The garage and front door to the house faced the street. The basement, finished off a few years ago by his grandpa (his mom's dad) and his dad, emptied out into a big backyard at the bottom of the hill. Toby's parents had moved to the Minneapolis area from Arizona when Toby was little to be close to Grandpa and Grandma Baxter. Toby had no memories of Arizona, although he, inspired by and along with his dad, cheered for the Arizona sports teams.

Toby parked his bike in the garage and ran into the house. He could smell the fresh baked cookies as he opened the door. His mom knew he loved chocolate chip cookies made with chocolate cookie dough. She always had them hot and ready every Friday after school.

With two cookies already stuffed into his mouth his mom asked him how his day was.

"Mnmnmnm," he mumbled, a few bits of cookie flying out of his mouth.

"Your dad will be home in an hour or so to help you decorate for the party. I know the last thing you want to do is homework, but you'll be busy all day tomorrow with your birthday party. And on Sunday Grandma Baxter is coming over for birthday breakfast. So, after you're done with your cookies, why don't you go into your room and spend twenty minutes reading from *The Hobbit*. Robin, I mean Mrs Grayson, said you need to read through chapter three by Monday."

Inconvenient!

After Toby wolfed down five cookies and a glass of milk he headed to his bedroom, which was through the door right off the kitchen. He loved his room. His bed sat next to the window, which looked down on the backyard. The yard was big enough to play soccer, with two acorn trees at the end of the yard standing like a pair of goal posts. The neighbors to the right had a big fence around their yard, which was a good thing because they had two mean dogs. They'd lost a few soccer balls to those dogs. To the left the yards gradually moved up the hill with no fences, providing lots of space for hide and seek. At the end of the backyard the neighbor behind them had installed a small chain-link fence with bushes all along it to provide a bit of privacy and to stop flying soccer balls.

Toby's room was fairly small but big enough for a single bed, a nightstand, a dresser, and a little desk for doing homework. It had a small closet that held some of his clothes and lots of his stuff. The room had two doors, one leading into the kitchen and the other into the bathroom hallway. The walls were covered with *Spider-Man* posters. His dad's friend managed the local Cineplex at the mall. He usually gave Toby's dad the *Spider-Man* movie posters once the movies were done with their first run. Toby had two of the Toby McGuire movie posters, one of the Andrew Garfield posters (autographed!) and the Tom Holland *Homecoming* poster. He had room for one or two more if he got creative.

His pride and joy, however, were the bookshelves attached to the wall over his desk, piled high with *Marvel* comic books. At last count he had over 150, collected over the last five years. He'd read every one of them, most of them many times, to make sure he was keeping up with the various storylines. He felt himself being pulled toward the latest *Captain America* comic book, but he resisted the temptation. He had work to do before his dad got home.

He pulled *The Hobbit* out of his backpack and sat down on his bed, propped up by *Thor* and *Black Panther* pillows. He opened the book, sighed, and began to read. More accurately, he skimmed and skipped his way through the assigned pages.

Until he got to the part describing hobbits. Hobbits, according to Tolkien, were about half the height of humans, with larger stomachs and shoeless feet covered with curly hair!

Toby stopped reading. His mind raced back to the little boy—man—he'd seen in front of his school a few hours ago. He kind of looked like the hobbit he'd just read about. In fact, although Toby had never seen *The Lord of the Rings* movies, that little boy—or man—did look like Frodo from the movie posters and trailers. But it couldn't be. Hobbits don't exist.

Out of the corner of his eye he noticed a shadow move across the window. He looked up and what he saw so shocked him that he fell off of the bed. He slowly lifted up his head to look out the window again, and there it was. A huge face. Not a scary face. But a big, huge face. Whatever body was holding up that head had to be at least nine-feet tall!

The face had a dark brown, closely-trimmed beard. Brown hair streaked with grey fell down around the face and just above the eyes. As Toby raised up his eyes he could see that the big head with the big face was wearing what seemed to be a Christmas wreath.

Toby cautiously stood up and climbed back onto the bed. The giant, if that's what it was, was wearing a green cloak of some sort with a white collar. And he was smiling. A genuinely big, warm smile, as if the giant were happy to see him.

Toby stared at the giant. The giant stared back at Toby with big, Christmas-green eyes.

Toby opened his mouth to speak but nothing came out. The giant continued to smile at him. The smile made him feel safe for some reason. Calm. Like everything was going to be OK.

Finally, *Mom!* exploded from Toby's lips. His mom rushed into the room.

"What's wrong, Toby? Toby, what's wrong?"

The only thing Toby could do was point at the window. His mom looked but all she could see was their beautiful backyard. The giant was gone.

"Toby, what is it? What's wrong, dear?"

Toby looked at her and finally said, "Sorry mom, I thought I saw a red Cardinal. I know how much you like them and I wanted you to see it."

Mom gave her son a big warm smile, much like the giant had done.

"Thank you, Toby." As she walked out the door she paused. "It smells like Christmas in here. Did you use some sort of fragrance spray?"

Toby simply smiled at her. It did smell like Christmas in his room. The smell of Christmas trees and Christmas cookies.

Toby shook his head, walked over to his bookshelf, and pulled down a *Black Panther* comic book. He needed to get his brain back together. It had been a weird few hours.

But just then he heard his dad's voice. Toby ran out into the kitchen and gave his dad a big hug.

"What's that all about Toby?" his dad asked.

"It's time to start decorating for the party!" Toby replied.

His dad told him to run to the car and get the bags out of the trunk. All the decorations were there. And, his dad told him, there was a little surprise as well.

As he was heading into the garage, he heard his dad say to his mom, "Does it smell like Christmas in here?"

Toby carried in three large bags of props and decorations for the party along with a poster tube. The surprise his dad hinted at had to be in that tube.

Toby placed the bags on the kitchen counter but held onto the tube.

"Go ahead, son," his dad said. "Open it!"

Toby impatiently ripped away the tape at the end of the tube and pulled off the plastic cover. It took a few moments to get the poster out of the tube but it was worth the wait. A new movie poster. *The Amazing Spider-Man: Far From Home,* autographed by Tom Holland! Toby knew just the spot for it. He ran by his dad, giving him a huge grin and a high five, and into his bedroom. He hung his new poster on the ceiling above his bed. Perfect.

Over the next few hours Toby was so busy decorating for the party, eating pizza with his parents, and helping mom bake *The Avengers* cupcakes that he forgot about the little boy/man and the Christmas giant.

Around nine pm he put on his *Spider-Man* pajamas and climbed into bed. He knew he was probably too old now to wear super hero pajamas but he didn't care. After all, who would see him? And they were so well worn that anything new would feel scratchy and uncomfortable.

He picked up *The Hobbit* and started reading.

But he struggled to keep his eyes open.

He sighed.

He yawned.

Toby Baxter fell asleep.

CHAPTER 2

"My Pajamas Aren't Waterproof!"

Toby!

Toby!

Toby Baxter!

Toby heard the voice from deep within a dream. He felt someone shaking his foot. Someone—or something—was trying to wake him up. But he didn't want to wake up.

Toby Baxter. Wake up old boy!

Finally, Toby opened his eyes. He was facing the window and could tell it was pitch dark outside. At the foot of the bed something was glowing.

As Toby's eyes adjusted to the light, he could see a man sitting in his desk chair. The man had a rather oval-shaped head—completely bald. *Shaved maybe?* He had dark eye-brows over bright green eyes and a well-groomed but slightly graying goatee. His hands were made for basketball. He wore jeans, a denim shirt, and a leather vest over the shirt. Around his neck hung what looked like reading glasses. In his large right hand he held a book and in the left hand a pencil.

Toby watched as the man sat back in his chair and crossed his legs. He was a tall man. He was also quite old. Toby guessed 45-50? His smile suggested that he was glad to see that Toby was awake.

Toby Baxter. So very good to meet you.

The man's lips moved. Toby could hear the words. But there it was again. The words appeared above the man's head as he said them.

Toby couldn't tell if he was actually hearing the man speak or simply reading the words and somehow the words were coming alive. Or both.

"Who are you and what are you doing in my bedroom and are you real or am I dreaming?"

Good questions, Toby. My name is Author.

As he said his name he gave a slight bow.

"Sorry, did you say Author or Arthur?"

Author.

He gave another slight bow.

"Author? Is that your name or is that what you do?"

Both.

Author chuckled as he answered. He had a deep, soothing voice.

Toby knew he should be freaking out right about now with a man sitting in his room, but nothing about the situation seemed threatening. Just... strange!

"What kind of stories do you write?"

Human stories. All different kinds of human stories. In fact, I'm working on one now.

Author put on his reading glasses, took up his pencil and scribbled a note in his book.

"Why are there words above your head when you speak?"

Author looked above his head.

Are there?

"Don't you see them?" Toby asked. "When you speak, the words you say appear above your head like in a comic book."

Author grinned to himself, made another note in his book, and then smiled at Toby.

Your probably wondering why I'm here.

Toby pointed to the spot just above Author's head. Author looked up and then back at Toby, puzzled.

"You said, *Your* probably wondering why I'm here. You should have said, *You're* probably wondering why I'm here."

Author ignored Toby's attempt to correct his grammar.

Did you see a—how shall I put it?—a small interesting looking man today?

Toby had nearly forgotten about that. He nodded yes. "I also saw a friendly giant who looks and smells like Christmas."

Author seemed genuinely surprised and pleased at that and made another note.

That little man needs your help.

"My help? Why my help? I'm just a kid."

Author paused for a moment and then started looking around the room.

"What're you looking for?"

Where's your wardrobe?

"Why do we need my clothes?"

No, not that kind of wardrobe. A wardrobe can also be a big cupboard-like piece of furniture that functions like a closet.

"I don't have one of those. I only have a closet. To you're left."

That's your left.

"No, it's to my right! Anyway, why do you need a wardrobe?"

Perhaps you've heard of the book, The Lion, The Witch, and the Wardrobe? The story of Narnia? Aslan the lion? The Pevensie children? Their adventures through the wardrobe?

Toby had heard about a movie with that title but hadn't seen it.

"I don't read books," Toby said before he could stop himself.

Author let out a huge laugh. A laugh so big it rattled the whole bedroom. Toby hoped it didn't wake his parents.

But you do read comic books, right?

Author pointed with his pencil to the comic books piled on the shelves behind him.

Toby nodded.

Those count, don't they?

Toby liked this guy, even if he was just a dream.

Author frowned.

What were we talking about?

"You were looking for a wardrobe but I don't have one. Why do you need it?"

Seems like a great way to jump into a story.

Toby stared at him, waiting for more. Author looked over at the closet, made a note, took off his glasses, and loudly closed the book as he put the pencil behind his ear.

Never mind. The closet will have to do. Come on.

"Come on where?"

Into your story, of course.

Intrigued and, quite honestly, thinking he was dreaming, Toby climbed out of bed and followed Author into the closet and out into…

… a pouring rainstorm. Within seconds Toby's *Spider-Man* pajamas were soaked. He turned to find Author standing next to him, completely clothed in raingear.

"Why didn't you tell me I needed a raincoat?" Toby shouted at him through the wind and pelting rain.

Author didn't seem to hear him. He was checking his pockets for something.

Toby scanned the area as best he could. Behind them was a rock-like wall with a hole that presumably led back to his bedroom.

To his right was a huge waterfall, adding to the drenching rain. To his left he could just make out a river bounded by hills and trees.

Directly in front of him was a small rock bridge over the river. Author was crossing it. He stopped and waved for Toby to follow him.

Toby could barely see with the wind-swept rain blowing in his face. They crossed the bridge and looked up the hill a bit. Again, it was hard to see, but there was something behind the trees. A big stone with something in the middle of it.

Author pulled a flashlight out of his raincoat and shone it onto the stone. Toby put his hands above his eyes to block out the pelting rain. It took a moment to take in what he was seeing. Embedded in the middle of the stone was a great… big… sword.

"Is… that… the… Sword in the Stone? King Arthur's… Excalibur?"

"Actually, King Arthur didn't pull Excalibur from the stone. That was a different sword. The Lady in the Lake gave him Excalibur," Author shouted.

Toby noticed that the words no longer appeared above Author's head when he spoke. He'd have to ask about that later. Right now he simply wanted to know why he was out in his pajamas in the middle of a rainstorm in the middle of who knows where, looking at the Sword in the Stone.

"Look more closely, Toby Baxter," Author said.

Toby leaned forward and noticed writing on the stone.

I.C.E. Call Toby Baxter.

Toby stepped backwards and almost fell over.

"What does it mean?" Toby shouted at Author.

"This is your destiny, Toby Baxter. This is your moment. This world needs you to pull your Sword from the stone and save them."

Toby had a million questions racing around in his head. *This world? What does he mean by This World? Where am I? And why me? I'm just a kid? What can I do to save a world?*

But he felt something drawing him to the Sword. Against his will he moved closer and closer until he found himself standing on the top of the stone.

Before he knew it, his hands were on the Sword.

Instantly several things happened at once.

The stone, the Sword, and Toby began to glow. He felt a surge of energy filling his entire body. His ears started ringing with what sounded like a hurricane in his head. He began pulling on the Sword… and it started to move! As it did, he heard a loud voice in his head trying to break through the light and the energy and the rain and the hurricane noise:

How will you use your power?

Toby recognized the voice. It was Grandpa Baxter. But how could that be? Grandpa Baxter died when Toby was three years old. He couldn't possibly remember his grandpa's voice. And yet he knew in the depth of his soul that Grandpa Baxter was speaking to him.

How will you use your power?

Toby continued to pull on the Sword. It moved perhaps an inch.

How will you use your power?

The voice grew louder. The hurricane in his mind howled more violently. The energy surging through him was about to explode when…

… everything stopped. The rain. The wind. The noise. The voice. The energy. The light.

Author stood next to him ready to catch him.

And then… the most vile, horrific, frightening howl Toby had ever heard ripped through the sudden quiet. It went on for a least a minute. Toby was glad his pajamas were already soaked because he was pretty sure he'd wet his pants.

"What was that?"

"Trolls!" Author said as he nervously glanced around.

"Trolls? Like those cute little dolls with the bright hair you buy at Target?"

"No!"

And that *No!* from Author was even more chilling than the troll howl.

Toby Baxter collapsed.

He suddenly sat up. He was in his bed. He was now in dry *Black Panther* pajamas. It was still dark outside and inside.

"Toby…" Author was back at the end of the bed, glowing.

Toby jumped. "What… what just happened? Was that real?" he asked.

"Toby, you're going to get a visit from that little man."

"I'd really rather not."

"Listen to him, Toby. He and his people need your help. They will explain everything. I must leave you now."

"Wait. Hold on…" Toby had so many questions that he couldn't articulate any of them. Finally, he sputtered out: "Why did the words stop appearing above your head?"

Author smiled, made a note in his book, and said, "That's the joy of reading a good book, Toby Baxter. Before you know it, the words disappear and suddenly your… you're… immersed in the story."

As Author turned to leave he asked, "Toby Baxter, how will you use your power?"

CHAPTER 3

Toby Baxter Turns 13

"Knock! Knock! Knock! Is the birthday boy up?"

Why did moms always do that... knock on the door and say "knock" at the same time?

"Hey, mom, yup. I'm just getting up. I need to take a shower."

"OK, Toby. Your favorite breakfast will be ready in half an hour."

Toby was taller than most of the kids in his class. He'd gone through a growth spurt during sixth grade and now stood about five-foot-seven inches tall. He plowed through three shoes sizes last year and the same in clothing sizes. He had a hard time finding pants that fit his skinny frame.

As his body changed, so did his voice. While he and his friend, Drew, were practicing their duet for the sixth-grade spring concert, Toby's voice cracked on a high note and he was never able to hit that note again. His Adam's apple was coming along quite nicely, thank you very much!

Because of his height Toby played basketball both at school and in his church league. He wasn't very good but he enjoyed the game and hanging with the other guys.

He also played trumpet in the band. That he was better at. In sixth grade he'd been the first chair trumpet. Jr. High was a bit different as he was competing against eighth graders. But he was holding his own.

Perhaps the biggest change in sixth grade: girls! Up until then he always saw girls as a nuisance to be tolerated. Then he noticed Rainie. She was funny. She was good at sports. And she was cute. But he never had the courage to talk to her and now she attended a different school.

One of his favorite things to do with his dad was to manage their annual Fantasy Football Team. They worked together on the draft each season and carefully followed their players throughout the year. Thankfully they had help from the *Fantasy Footballers Podcast*. And of course, Sunday afternoons were spent watching the *Arizona Cardinals*.

As he looked himself in the mirror getting ready to take a shower, he admired the growing peach fuzz on his face. Another few years and he would be shaving! He had a few freckles on his face and no pimples—yet—but he knew they were coming. His hair was a deep auburn, thick and wavy. His mom's friends told him that they would pay lots of money to have hair like his. He had no idea what they were talking about.

Today he was turning thirteen. It seemed like a big deal. A teenager!

His dad had taken him out for a *Dad and Son* dinner chat on Thursday. Toby feared it would be another one of those awkward birds and bugs… *or was it bees?*… conversations. But his dad wanted to talk about something deeper.

They sat across from each other in a booth at *Dairy Queen*. Toby wolfed down a bacon double cheeseburger, a large order of fries, and an extra-large root beer. He topped it off with a *Triple Chocolate Utopia* with chocolate ice cream—a *Quadruple Chocolate Utopia!*

"I brought you here to ask you something important, Toby," his dad began.

Uh oh… Toby thought. *Here it comes…*

"What kind of a man do you want to be, Toby?"

"Huh?" Toby mumbled through a mouthful of ice cream. The question had caught him off guard. He was expecting his dad to ask, "Do you know how your body works?" or something similarly embarrassing and uncomfortable.

What kind of man do I want to be? he thought. *I'm not even thirteen yet!*

"My dad asked me that very question when I turned thirteen," his dad said. "He wanted to make sure, as I entered my teen years, that I was making the kinds of decisions that would set me up to be a good man. How will you use your talents and gifts and passions, Toby? How will you use your power?"

"What power are you talking about, Dad?" Toby asked. But his dad suddenly seemed lost in thought. He was staring off into the distance, rubbing the top of his right hand with his left, as if he were somewhere else.

He watched his dad for what felt like several minutes, not wanting to interrupt him, but curious about what his dad was "seeing."

"Dad… Dad… Are you OK?"

Shaking his head, his dad said, "Sorry, Toby, when I asked you how you would use your power I was reminded of something important from when I was your age… but I couldn't quite get it." He paused again for a moment. "Oh well, it's gone now."

At that moment the door to *Dairy Queen* flew open and in walked four boys, laughing and punching each other. One of them spotted Toby.

Toby groaned.

"What is it, Toby?" his dad asked.

Before Toby could answer the group walked over to their booth.

The leader of the group patted Toby on the back, a bit too hard, and said, "Hey, guys, it's our friend Toby Baxter! Hello, Toby!"

Toby kept his eyes glued to the table in front of him. "Hello, Derrick," he muttered.

"This must be your father. So nice to meet you, Mr Baxter. Toby here is a good friend of ours." The other boys stifled their laughter.

To his horror Toby watched as his dad gave Derrick a great big smile, reached out his hand and said, "Nice to meet you. Derrick is it?" Derrick tentatively shook his hand.

"You boys look hungry. Here, take this. Dessert's on me. Thanks for being friends with Toby."

Toby watched, this time stunned, as his dad handed Derrick a $20 bill.

But then… a moment of surprise. Derrick was caught speechless. He wasn't sure what to do. His usual cockiness was gone! Derrick looked at his friends seemingly for support. They all shrugged. Then he sheepishly took the $20 and mumbled his thanks. Without saying another word, Derrick and his friends headed to the counter and placed their orders.

Toby's dad looked at Toby for several moments.

"You aren't really friends, are you," his dad said with a smile.

Toby had never told his parents about Derrick. Derrick is in eighth grade. A couple of times Toby and his friend Sid had been on the receiving end of Derrick's "just having a little fun with you guys" bad sense of humor. They had learned to avoid him.

Toby's dad looked over at Derrick and his friends and waved, causing further discomfort for Derrick. "Your friend Derrick doesn't know what hit him," his dad said, laughing.

Then he pulled something out of his pocket. "This is the other reason why I brought you here tonight, Toby. I want to give you a gift. For generations, even centuries, dads have been giving something like this to their sons when they turn thirteen. This particular gift traces itself back to a Jewish sage."

"Sage? Isn't that a spice?"

"Actually, it's an herb. But in this case we're talking about sage, as in a wise man, philosopher, and teacher by the name of Gurion.

"My grandpa—your great grandpa—gave this to my dad when my dad turned thirteen. My dad—your grandpa—gave this to me when I turned thirteen. And now I want to give it to you. I've carried it with me since the day my dad gave it to me."

At that point Derrick and his buddies got up to leave. Just as he was about to walk out the door, Derrick turned and gave a slight nod to Toby and his dad.

Toby's dad waved at Derrick, then turned back to Toby and handed him a well-worn card, recently laminated. It pictured an ancient-looking hand-drawn map. Though the map wasn't very big Toby could make out what looked like a waterfall pouring into a stream leading to a river. The stream was lined on one side by a high wall or cliff, and a path on the other. An arrow pointed to a spot that said, *Start Here,* with a dotted line leading downstream.

"I don't get it," Toby said. "I can see that it's a map, but a map to where?"

"Turn the card over, Toby."

Toby did so and saw another old-looking hand drawing, this time of a compass. But rather than N-E-S-W as the coordinates, the compass had H-E-R-O with these words beneath it:

H=Honorable. *Do the right thing. Always.*

E=Enterprising. *Find a way forward.*

R=Responsible. *Use your gifts and abilities in the service of others.*

O=Original. *Be yourself.*

Toby held the card in his hands like a sacred gift, which it was. "What does it mean?" he asked.

"It may not feel like it, Toby, but your thirteenth birthday marks the time-honored starting point of your journey into manhood. This small card serves as a map and a compass of sorts, reminding you to make wise decisions as you grow up, decisions that will help you become a heroic man. That's my dream for you, son, that you grow to be a good man." He paused for a moment before continuing.

"And Toby, I also want to say something very important to you that my dad said to me when I was turning thirteen. I'm proud of you! I'm glad you're my son. I love you and always will."

Now, standing in front of the mirror and remembering that important time with his dad, Toby practiced his "man face." Then he headed into the shower.

He stopped for a moment. *How will you use your power?* His dad had asked him that question at their special dinner Thursday night. But he felt like he had just heard that same question recently.

He scratched his head. He couldn't get it. Oh well. His stomach was growling, ready for his favorite breakfast: Chicken sausages and chocolate chip pancakes made with chocolate pancake batter. He threw off his *Black Panther* pajamas—*wait a minute, wasn't he wearing his Spider-Man pajamas last night?*—and headed to the shower.

Breakfast was as delicious as Toby hoped it would be. His mom and dad gave him another present (in addition to the Tom Holland autographed *Spider-Man* poster): a gift card worth $50 to his favorite comic book store. If he didn't have friends coming over soon for the party he would have hopped on his bike and headed straight to the comic book store right then.

Just as he was putting on his *Spider-Man* gloves to complete his costume, the doorbell rang. He threw on his *Spidey* mask and answered the door. It was the *Black Panther* (his new friend, Sid), along with *Captain Marvel* (Lori), *Thor* (Bruce), *Iron Man* (Drew), *Black Widow* (Lise), *Captain*

America (Jeff) and *Ant-Man* (Dave). The rest of the group arrived within minutes of each other.

They headed to the backyard where Toby and his dad had set up the games. First up: *Super Hero Corn Hole.* Toby's mom had ordered it online. The beanbags featured different super heroes. Toby won the playoff. He wasn't sure if he was really that good or if his friends had let him win.

They played *Pin the Cape on Thor* followed by a two-team relay race that included eggs, spoons, running, and lots of screaming and laughing.

Then it was the time for gifts. The heroes headed into the house, but as Toby turned to shut the door, he saw a movement by the trees in the back of the yard. He closed the door behind him and slowly walked in that direction. At first he didn't see anything, but then he caught the movement again in the bushes. Toby took a tentative step or two closer when a head appeared, popping out of the bushes. It was the same curly haired boy/man he had seen at school the day before. In the busyness of his birthday he had put the boy/man out of his mind.

The boy/man cautiously stepped out of the bushes. It was apparent close up that this was no boy. This was a man. He stood about seven inches shorter than Toby. He had deep brown eyes with eyebrows that angled up and away from the top of his nose. His ears were pointy at the top, sticking over the Arizona Diamondbacks Baseball cap he was wearing. *A baseball cap... on a guy who looks kind of like a hobbit?*

Toby Baxter, we need your help.

The voice was the deep voice of a man. And once again, the words were printed above his head.

"Who are you why do you need me are you a hobbit?" The questions spilled out of Toby as one long sentence.

My name is Deckor. I don't have time to answer your questions right now. Trust me. We need you. Tonight...

"Toby! Hey Toby! Who are you talking to? Or, is it, To whom are you talking?" It was *Black Panther*/Sid calling down to him from the kitchen window. Toby had quickly discovered in his short friendship with him that Sid struggled with grammar just as he did (or is it just *like* he did?). Toby turned to look at Sid and then back to Deckor but Deckor was gone.

"No one!" Toby shouted back to Sid. Toby ran into the house through the basement door and raced up the stairs to the kitchen, where everyone was already devouring hotdogs and lemonade.

Once all of the super heroes were stuffed, they headed into the living room to open gifts. Twelve boxes of various sizes sat in the middle of the room. But just as Toby was about to dive into his birthday presents, the doorbell rang.

"It must be someone to see you, Toby," his mom said.

Toby ran to the door, opened it, and groaned. It was his dad, not so cleverly disguised as *Batman*. At least, Toby thought, he was trying to be *Batman*. The suit wasn't black or armor-like like the Michael Keaton or Christian Bale *Batman* suits. This one was made of blue tights and a long-sleeved blue t-shirt with dark blue wrestling or boxer shorts over the tights. The cowl and cape, like the boxer shorts, were made of some sort of shiny material. A cheap yellow "Utility Belt" was wrapped around Dad's waist. Not a *Batman* who would inspire fear in the hearts of Gotham's most vile criminals. His dad said something about the best and original *Batman* played by some guy named Adam West, but no one knew whom he was talking about—*or was it "who" he was talking about?*

Dad-*Batman* was a huge hit with the other super heroes as he highfived them one by one. Toby, however, wasn't sure it was right to have a *DC* hero mixing with *Marvel* heroes. Dad-*Batman* didn't seem to care and took the lead in handing the birthday gifts to him one at a time.

Even though all of the presents were of different sizes, after gift four it was apparent that all of the super heroes were in on the joke. Every present was a gift card worth $10 to the comic book store. And Toby couldn't have been happier!

Then it was back to the food table for the best part of the day: *Avenger* cupcakes and ice cream. Being a chocolate fan, Toby had chosen a triple layer chocolate cupcake recipe along with chocolate cookies-and-cream ice cream. Chocolate marshmallows, chocolate chips, and a thick, dark chocolate sauce were on hand to be added at will. And all of the super heroes willed!

Suddenly his dad said, "Does it smell like Christmas to anyone else?"

Bruce-*Thor* laughed. "I'm Jewish. How would I know what Christmas smells like! But now that you mention it, it does smell like the mall in December."

Toby wasn't laughing. "I need to run to the bathroom," he said and took off downstairs. He ran to the door leading to the backyard. As he opened it he was met by two legs, supporting the giant he had seen the day before. The smell of Christmas was strong. He had an urge to start singing *Jingle Bells*.

Toby headed outside, ducking under the legs of the giant. "What do you want?" he asked.

The giant bent down and flashed a big warm smile at Toby. Toby was filled with a sense… of joy… of calm… of… of… of… he couldn't quite put his finger on it. But whatever it was it felt good deep down inside.

"Who are you? Are you with that little man? Why do you smell like Christmas? Why can't anyone else see you but only smell you?"

"Toby? Toby? Is everything alright down there?" It was *Batman*-Dad.

Toby rushed into the house and quietly shut the door.

"I'm good, Dad. It took me a minute to get back into my *Spider-Man* costume."

His dad, standing on the bottom step of the basement, was sniffing the air. "Toby, does it smell like Christmas to you? It reminds me of something…"

"Christmas?" asked Toby.

Toby's dad had that far-away look in his eyes again, as if he had been transported to another time. After a minute he looked at Toby and returned to the present.

"Your friends are ready to head home. Let's go up and thank them for a great party."

Toby quickly looked outside through the basement door window but the giant was gone.

It had been a long, fun, crazy day. A birthday party. Gifts. Food. A guy who looks like a hobbit. A giant who smells like Christmas. His dad was right. Turning thirteen was a big deal.

Toby said goodnight to his parents after thanking them for a great birthday party and closed the door to his bedroom. He opened the dresser drawer to grab his *Spidey* pajamas. They were soaking wet! How did that happen?

Suddenly a memory… a man holding a book and pencil… the closet… a drenching rainstorm… a waterfall… a sword… *How will you use your power?* It had been a dream, right?

Toby hung the wet pajamas on a couple of hangers from the closet so they could dry out. He put on his *Black Panther* pajamas, climbed into bed, turned off the light and quickly fell asleep.

CHAPTER 4

Back into the Closet

Toby Baxter! Toby Baxter! Wake up! We need to go!

Toby had been in a deep, dreamless sleep. It took him several seconds after forcing his eyes open to realize that that little man was back, now at the foot of his bed, trying to wake him up. *What was his name again? Dickle? Dacman? Dustin?*

Deckor!

There were the words again, above Deckor's head.

"How did you know what I was… never mind. Go away! Let me sleep! You're not real!" Toby turned over, closed his eyes, and wrapped his pillow around his head.

He felt the pillow ripped from his arm and a hand on his shoulder shaking him.

Toby Baxter! We must go. Now! It's your time!

Toby sat up. "I'm not going anywhere until you answer my questions."

Not now, Toby Baxter. I'll answer them once we get to where we're going.

"I'm not going out in my pajamas again!"

Here. Put these on. They will protect you from rain, cold, heat, and arrows.

"Arrows?!"

Toby noticed, as Deckor threw the clothes at him, that Deckor had a green line on his right hand that ran from his wrist to his middle knuckle. Before Toby could ask about it Deckor said:

Put them on! Now!

Deckor's tone had changed. He was getting impatient.

Toby changed into the clothes. They were dark green, and seemingly made of leather. Pants, a tunic, a pair of soft but firm boots, and a dark green hooded cloak, with a touch of yellow.

Let's go. Follow me!

Toby headed back into his small closet, this time following Deckor.

A moment later he walked out into blinding sunshine.

He couldn't believe the difference from the night before. It was warm, but not hot. The breeze was gentle. A perfect summer day. *Wait a minute. How is that possible? It's fall, isn't it?*

The sound of the waterfall to his right was almost hypnotic. He watched as Deckor stood with his face toward the sky, his eyes closed, drinking in the sunlight.

Toby used that moment to get his bearings. He remembered the steep stone cliff/hill behind him, which somehow provided a way in and out of his closet. The waterfall to his right flowing, not into a river, as he had assumed last night, but into a large stream. Across the stream was the small bridge made of rocks, leading to a path that ran to his left down along the stream. The stream was bordered by trees of various shapes and sizes. It smelled fresh and clean. *Maybe this is what nature smells like?*

He looked up the hill on the other side of the stream, searching for the Sword in the stone. But he was shocked to see that the stone monument holding the Sword had been broken into pieces and that the Sword was gone!

As he tried to take in the missing Sword he felt Deckor staring at him. Deckor turned to see what Toby was looking at. Deckor opened his mouth as if he were about to say something about the Sword when…

… they heard that horrific, blood-curdling, terrifying screech and scream that rang out the night before.

Deckor yelled, **Trolls**! and ran over the bridge and down the path, pulling out a sword from a sheath on his side. A horn sounded in the distance, downstream.

Toby stood stunned for a moment, and then began to run after Deckor. He'd lost sight of Deckor immediately but thankfully there was only one path and it followed the stream. The screeching continued and everything in Toby told him to run back the other way, into the hole in the wall, and into the safety of his bedroom. But he kept running toward the scream and the blaring horn.

After running for several minutes Toby found himself in an open area. The stream had formed a small pond before it continued its journey to wherever it was going. Trees surrounded the pond like a canopy. Toby saw people the size of Deckor running seemingly all over the place, some grabbing children—*were they children?*—and running into holes in the face of the rock wall, others running out of those holes with arrows and swords.

Then the screeching stopped, thankfully. Everyone looked around—up the stream, down the stream, up the cliff wall, over at the other side of the pond toward what looked like a ball field—as if waiting for some horrifying monster to appear. After a few tense moments everyone seemed to relax. People tentatively peeped out of their hiding holes to make sure all was safe. Then, as if nothing had happened, the villagers went back to their business of drawing water, washing clothes, cooking meals, sharpening swords, and playing with the kids.

Soon people noticed him. How could they not? He stood at least seven inches taller than the rest of them. And he didn't have big hairy feet.

Then he heard whispers:

"Who is that, Daddy?"

"Is that Toby Baxter?"

"Is he the one who has come to help us?"

"He's just a boy!"

He felt a hand grab his right arm at the elbow. "Come with me," Deckor said. "This way."

Deckor led him to a fire pit near the far end of the pond. Sitting on wood benches were two females and two males. Though they were on the short side like Deckor, they were obviously adults. A fifth person was tending to one of the males and one of the females who had been wounded. As he did so he quietly hummed a song. Toby could feel healing energy as he listened to it. He felt his fear quickly disappearing.

"Toby Baxter, meet my family."

The two males and the two females looked up at Toby with a mixture of awe, surprise, and... *was it disappointment?*

"This is my older sister, Clovor." Clovor was in some pain due to the wound on her knee. "She is the leader—or leader in the making—of our village."

Clovor looked to be about four-and-a-half-feet tall. She had long, curly brown hair and rich, deep, brown eyes. Her eyebrows angled upward from the bridge of her nose, like Deckor's, rather than curving over the top of her eyes like his own did. Her ears seemed to be pointed at the top, but it was hard to tell as they were covered by her long hair. Like her brother Deckor she had rather large, hairy feet. Her clothing was similar to what Toby was wearing, although her pants were covered by a small skirt. Her arms were exposed. And ripped! On her back was a bow along with a quiver of arrows. She bowed slightly from the waist to Toby, and then returned her focus to the medic as he worked on her knee.

"This is my older brother, Phoenix."

Like Deckor, Phoenix had brown curly hair that spilled down his face, over his apparently pointy ears, and down his neck. He stood about five feet tall and also had the big hairy feet. His eyebrows, too, angled up from the bridge of the nose. His eyes were deep brown like Clovor's. On his side Phoenix wore a sheath with a long sword in it, long for a person his size, anyway. Like Deckor, he too, had the green line on his right hand. Toby couldn't tell if Clovor had a similar mark as she was wearing her archery gloves. And, to Toby's surprise, rather than a leather tunic, Phoenix wore a #13 Arizona Cardinal's jersey with *Warner* printed on the back of it. Phoenix noticed Toby staring at his jersey.

"One of the greatest quarterbacks of all time! I had the good fortune of being at the Big Game in February of 2009, your world's time. Raymond James Stadium in Tampa…"

"You mean the Super…" Phoenix quickly jumped up and clamped his hand over Toby's mouth.

"You can't say that!"

"Can't say what? Super…" Again the hand clamp over Toby's mouth. Phoenix looked around nervously.

"You can't say Super blah blah blah or you-know-who will hit you up with a fine."

"Who and what are you talking about? That's not true," Toby said. "We say Super…" For the third time a hand clamp. "We say it all the time…" he mumbled through Phoenix's fingers.

"Google it!" Phoenix said, as if that settled it.

"Anyway, the Cardinals had taken the lead with a Kurt Warner to Larry Fitzgerald pass with about two minutes and twenty seconds to go in the game…" Phoenix stopped talking and stared off into space as if reliving the moment.

Toby was a huge football fan. He'd heard the stories about that particular game. It was Cardinals' lore in his family. His grandpa had managed to snag tickets and saw it in person.

Phoenix suddenly seemed to remember where he was, jumped up to high-five Toby, and sat down, but not before noticing Deckor's baseball cap. He grabbed it off of his brother's head, put it onto his own and said, "Thanks for remembering!"

Deckor continued the introductions. "The one getting his face stitched up is my cousin, Judah."

Judah, unlike his cousins, had blond curly hair cut short, showing off his pointy ears. He had blue eyes and the same eyebrows as his cousins. Then it hit him. They looked like Mr Spock eyebrows from the J. J. Abrams' *Star Trek* movies. Judah had a disarming smile and walked over to shake Toby's hand. Judah's right hand had the green mark.

"We've been waiting for you for a long time." As Judah smiled he grabbed his cheek, still bleeding through the new stitches and dressing. The wound obviously hurt. Judah wore clothes similar to those of Deckor, with what appeared to be a small dagger sheath on each hip. He sat down as if dizzy.

"Finally, this is Judah's little sister, Mathilda. She prefers to be called MathilDAH!"

The others laughed. Apparently an in-the-family-joke. Mathilda had blond hair like her brother but it was long and curly, like Clovor's. She had bright blue eyes that immediately suggested she was a handful—like the fun Aunt. She ran up and gave Toby a big bear hug. Toby could feel the muscles in her arms through her long-sleeved leather tunic. She wore fingerless gloves, which he assumed was because she, too, was an archer.

What Toby found striking was how different the cousins were from each other. Clovor, Phoenix, and Deckor were dark of skin and features. Judah and Mathilda were light of skin and features.

"By the way, the person working on their wounds is the Healer."

The Healer, done with his work, headed up the stream to attend to more of the wounded. The five cousins sat down on the benches next to the pond. Clovor motioned for Toby to join them. A young male brought them something to drink. Toby looked into the wooden cup, smelled it, and sipped it. It was the freshest, cleanest water he had ever tasted. He swallowed it all in one gulp. He hadn't realized he was so thirsty.

The five cousins sat staring at him, almost as if to determine if he had the wherewithal to help them. He knew he didn't and they would surely find that out in a few moments.

"You probably have lots of questions for us, Toby Baxter, and we have many for you," Clovor said. And it was then that he noticed the words didn't form above her head. Apparently, he was back into the story.

CHAPTER 5

Toby Baxter Has Lots of Questions

"Who are you?" Toby asked. "And where am I? What is this place?"

"We are the River Elves," Judah answered. "And this is *RiverHome*."

"Wait! What? You're not hobbits? You look like hobbits! I was just reading about hobbits and you sure look like hobbits from the description in the book. Are you telling me you're not hobbits?"

"Nope. We're just your common, everyday River Elves." It was Phoenix who answered.

"But… your… your feet!"

Suddenly they were all laughing. Toby had no idea what he had said. Then Mathilda reached down and grabbed her left foot. And to Toby's surprise, she pulled it off! He thought he would faint until he realized that she had pulled a hairy boot off of her small, human-looking foot. "Best, most comfortable boots in all the worlds."

Worlds? thought Toby.

"And this is called *RiverHome* because you are River Elves?"

Mathilda giggled and said, "The force is strong with this one, Obi Wan!"

Toby knew it was a silly question as it was coming out of his mouth. But he didn't have time to be embarrassed because Mathilda apparently knew about *Star Wars*.

"How do you know…"

"About *Star Wars*?" Mathilda asked. "Because from time to time when we cross into your world for your help we pick up good books and good movies. I'm partial to the *Marvel* movies myself." She winked at Toby as if they were in on a conspiracy together. He liked her.

"Why am I here? What just happened here? How did you get those wounds? What's up with the trolls? What happened to the Sword in the stone?" The questions came out like word vomit. He couldn't help himself.

"Toby Baxter, these questions are best answered over a meal," Judah said. "You must be hungry." And he was! He was starving.

Then it struck him. There had been a deluge just hours ago but no trace of rain. Everything was dry. None of the trees seemed to have lost their leaves from the violent wind.

"Why don't I see any puddles from the rainstorm last night?"

Deckor looked at him, trying to figure out the question. Then his face lit up.

"I remember that storm! It happened about six months ago. The trolls tried to attack us but an energy burst near the waterfall scared them off. Was that you, Toby Baxter?"

"Six months ago… but it was only last night?"

"It's a timey wimey thing, Toby Baxter. You have much to learn and we have much to tell you. Come and eat." Mathilda took him by the arm and led him down the path back in the direction of the waterfall, eventually bringing him into a hole in a cliff wall.

The hole was so small that even the River Elves had to bend down slightly to get in. Toby almost had to crawl in. But once through the small entrance, he found himself in a huge hall. It was obviously bigger on the inside! The hall was carved out of stone with a slight golden glow radiating from the rock walls. The numerous candle lights added to the glow and created a soothing warmth—a feeling of home. The hall seemed to serve both as a "family room" and the eating space. A long table sat—*do tables sit?*—in the middle of the hall with eleven high back chairs around it. Scattered throughout were what looked like leather beanbag chairs. Phoenix plopped down into one and promptly fell asleep.

A hallway led out of the main room opposite the entrance, and it looked as if doors lined it. Perhaps bedrooms. To the left of the long table was another doorway, which Toby guessed served as the entrance to the kitchen. To the right was a fireplace alive with fire.

The smell of fresh baked bread filled the hall. That, and something else... chicken? He couldn't quite tell but he realized again that he really was hungry.

Clovor approached him with a goblet. "Drink this," she commanded. But the light in her eyes suggested to him that she really wasn't forcing him to drink. It was an offer of hospitality.

"What is it?" Toby asked.

"Taste it."

Toby sniffed it. He took a sip. And within seconds he'd downed the whole goblet of whatever it was. The flavor was light—a hint of fresh squeezed orange perhaps. Whatever it was, he felt the effects of it from the top of his head to the bottom of his feet. It was like an energy drink but without the buzz.

"What is it?" Toby asked again.

"It's our secret River Elves concoction. We call it water with a hint of fresh squeezed orange." Clovor winked at him and motioned him to the table.

As they headed to the table Clovor kicked Phoenix, jarring him out of his nap. The five River Elves took their seats. Judah invited Toby to sit next to him.

An elderly couple walked out of the kitchen carrying plates of food. It took them several trips, but soon the table was filled with fresh bread, roasted sweet potatoes, chicken, and what looked like two different sauces. Goblets were filled with the River Elves concoction and passed around the table so each had one.

The elderly couple then joined them at the table. "These are our grandparents," Mathilda said. "They've raised us since we lost our parents in the Troll War, twenty-five of your years ago. You can call them Grandpa and Grandma, if you'd like."

Grandpa and Grandma smiled at Toby and as they did Toby heard the voice of his own grandfather: *How will you use your power?*

He looked around to find the source of the voice, only to discover that everyone was staring at him.

"Are you all right, Toby?" Grandma asked. Toby nodded yes.

The elves joined hands and bowed their heads. Judah took Toby's right hand and Grandma took his left. At first all was silent. Then Toby heard a low hum, like the hum he had heard earlier from the Healer. This time it was Grandpa. The humming grew in volume and Toby could feel its energy like electricity in his body.

Grandpa prayed: "O, Creator. For sparing my grandchildren today from the trolls, I give you thanks. For our new friend, Toby Baxter, we give you praise. And for this bounty of food, we are grateful." Then more humming, growing softer, until all was quiet. It seemed like an eternity of silence when Judah and Grandma finally let go of his hands and everyone dived into their meals, including Toby.

Toby hated sweet potatoes. But not today. Best sweet potatoes ever. He loved bread, especially this bread. And the chicken fell off the bones and melted in the mouth, enhanced by what had to be fruit sauces. The River Elves concoction washed it all down and settled his stomach.

Phoenix let out a huge burp. "Just making room for dessert."

The day had been filled with one surprise after another, and Toby was in for one more. Grandma walked out of the kitchen with a huge multi-layered chocolate cake with thirteen birthday candles on it.

"We know you recently celebrated your birthday, Toby!" she said. They all sang happy birthday to him and gave him a huge piece of the cake. He could have used one of Phoenix's big burps as his stomach was about to explode.

As the final plate was removed from the table Toby heard a knock at the door. It was the Healer, followed by two female and two male River Elves. Deckor introduced them.

"You've briefly met the Healer. This is Donold, Johanna, Ethol and Victor." The five of them bowed to Toby, shook his hand, and then took seats at the table. The five River Elf cousins sat back down and motioned for Toby to do the same. Grandpa and Grandma served them all piping hot cider.

"Toby Baxter," Clovor began, "those of us here tonight make up the *RiverHome* Council. It is our responsibility to keep *RiverHome* and its inhabitants safe from any and all who might want to attack, harm, or destroy us. In times of crisis we add an eleventh chair, the chair for the One who has been chosen to fight with us in such a time as this."

Fight? Such a time as this? What does that mean? They think I've been chosen to help them? OK, Toby. It's time to wake up.

All Toby could do was stare at them one by one.

"Why me?"

"That's a good question, Toby Baxter. Before we can answer it, we have a story to tell you."

CHAPTER 6

Before the Beginning

Once again the room was filled with a low humming. It was mesmerizing, but it also made Toby tired. In fact, he felt exhausted.

Judah began to tell a story. Yet "tell" wasn't the right word. It sounded more like he was singing it. The melody, if that's what it was, reminded Toby of Celtic music. *Why is it always Celtic music in these fantasy worlds?*

"Before time as we know it the Creator spoke. The Creator spoke 'Water!' and the seas and rivers were formed. The Creator spoke 'Land!' and valleys and mountains and hills sprang up out of the waters.

"The Creator spoke 'Water Creatures!' and the rivers and seas and lakes gave birth to fish and dolphins and whales and turtles and sea lions and seals.

"The Creator called for winged creatures to inhabit the sky and the sky was filled with birds and dragons and…"

"Wait! What? Dragons? There are dragons here? They fly? Are they dangerous? Do they breathe fire? Do they collect diamonds…?"

Judah ignored Toby's questions.

"Next, the Creator called out to the waters, drawing some of the sea creatures onto the land. As they left the waters the sea creatures morphed into land animals; lions, hippos, giraffes, griffins, unicorns, lizards, dogs, boars, monkeys..."

"OK, Judah," chided Mathilda. "We get the picture."

"Then the Creator gathered the Council of Heaven together and said, 'We need someone to represent us... someone to act as our viceroys in this new world.'"

"What's a viceroy?" Toby asked.

Phoenix answered. "According to Dictionary.com a viceroy is *a person appointed to rule a country or province as the deputy of the sovereign.*"

"How did you access Dictionary.com?"

Phoenix, like Judah had done a moment ago, ignored the question and picked up the story.

"So the Creator spoke and out of the ground emerged elves and giants and gnomes and ogres..."

"Giants? Gnomes? Ogres?" Toby asked.

"And trolls and humans...." Phoenix continued

"Humans? Like me?" *Or is it like I?*

"The Creator," Phoenix went on, "tasked them with caring for the world, protecting it, and keeping it healthy.

"For tens of thousands of years the creatures of the air, sea, and land lived in harmony..."

"Toby! Toby Baxter! Toby! Wake up!"

Toby looked around in a daze. Deckor was shaking him. He could feel drool on the side of his face and felt a small bump growing on his right cheek. Apparently he had fallen asleep and hit his face on the table. He was so tired he hadn't felt it. His mom always joked that he could sleep through a hurricane.

Grandma was at his side in a second with a nice, cool cloth to put over the growing bruise. Grandpa gave him another goblet of the River Elf concoction. Toby drank it and felt a new burst of energy.

"Sorry about that," he said.

Mathilda giggled at him but Clovor gave her a look of warning.

"We're the ones who are sorry, Toby Baxter," Clovor said. "We have not been good hosts. You are exhausted and this is a lot to take in. Would you like to call it a day and get back to the story after breakfast?"

Toby shook his head. He could tell the Council was eager to finish the story. And he still had no idea why he was here… wherever here was.

"Go on. The drink and the cool cloth help. And it's OK to call me Toby." He stood up, stretched, and sat back down ready to listen. As he did so the low humming restarted and Deckor took up the story… again with that Celtic kind of music.

"For tens of thousands of years the creatures of the land, sea, and air lived in harmony. Trolls, gnomes, ogres, elves, giants, humans and all the peoples of the earth lived as neighbors, tilling the land, sharing food, caring for one another's children, sharing stories.

"And then the Chaos descended over the earth. A darkness one could not see, only feel. A foreboding. A terror. A fear. An undefined sense of despair that slowly began to breed suspicion and distrust between neighbors. The trolls moved to the east. The ogres migrated south. The elves to the west. And the humans to the north. No one knew why. It was all instinct. The gnomes and their wolves play hide and seek, constantly on the move. We lose touch with them and then suddenly they show up for awhile. The giants have vanished off the face of the earth, we think.

"Over the centuries, as the groups grew increasingly distant from each other, distrust grew as well. They developed their own languages and customs. To survive they created unique homes to weather the elements.

"And as long as no one crossed territorial lines, peace seemingly held a tentative hold over the earth.

"In reality, that peace was a mirage. Violence and hatred were growing…"

Suddenly a loud clap of thunder rocked the elven home, instantly followed by the horrifying shrieking Toby had heard before. This time he could understand what the shrieking was saying:

TOBY BAXTER! TOBY BAXTER! GO HOME. YOU CANNOT SAVE THE ELVES. WE HAVE YOUR SWORD! YOUR MISSION IS A FAILURE. GO HOME, TOBY BAXTER. YOU ARE NOT A HERO!

The cousins leapt into action. Judah grabbed his daggers. Phoenix retrieved his sword. Clovor and Mathilda threw on their arrow-filled quivers and snatched up their bows.

"Trolls!" Deckor shouted as he ran into a room at the end of the hallway, returning with a huge sword and shield.

"Protect him!" Clovor nodded toward Toby who was now standing by the table, staring at the door, too paralyzed to move. Immediately Ethol, Johanna, and Victor flanked him, swords raised, ready to fight to the death for him.

The cousins, led by Donold and followed by the Healer, raced out the door. Grandpa locked the door behind them and he, along with Grandma, armed with bows and arrows, faced the door with their arrows aimed at it.

The shrieking continued, worming its way into Toby's mind, heart, and then soul. The life seemed to drain out of him. He felt cold… all alone… Still, he couldn't move.

TOBY BAXTER. YOU ARE NOT A HERO. GO HOME. YOU CANNOT HELP THE ELVES.

Then, just as quickly as it had started, everything went silent. Deathly silent. The silence seemed even more frightening than the screeching and shrieking.

No one moved. No one seemed to breathe. They all stood on high alert, listening… waiting… wondering…

Toby felt himself begin to shake. He couldn't help it. His body had taken over. Victor noticed that Toby was about to collapse onto the floor and grabbed him just in time. He led Toby over to the beanbag chair Phoenix had been napping in earlier. He eased Toby into it and immediately he, along with Ethol, and Johanna, surrounded Toby once again with swords raised.

Toby felt the tears starting to force themselves out of his eyes. He tried to keep them in but the uncontrollable shaking knocked them loose and soon he was crying. Not tears of sadness but tears of sheer panic. His body was in full-blown shock and he couldn't do anything about it. Snot ran from his nose. Tears ran down onto this leather tunic. Sweat poured out of every sweat producing area of his body. Toby Baxter was melting down. Some hero!

He didn't hear the coded knock on the door. He didn't see Grandma and Grandpa lower their bows and arrows and unlock the door. He didn't see Donold and the cousins and the Healer rush into the room. He didn't see his three guards lower their swords and move away. He didn't see Clovor kneel down beside him.

"Toby," she said softly. "Toby. Toby. Look at me."

"No!"

"Toby," she tried again. "Look at me."

"No. Go away. Leave me be. I'm no hero. I'm ashamed. I don't want you to see me like this."

"Why?"

"Why do you think? Heroes don't cry. For goodness' sake, boys don't cry."

Judah, Deckor, and Phoenix said a collective, "Uh-oh!"

Clovor swatted Toby across the head. "Who told you that? Who told you that boys don't cry?"

"Hey!" Toby said. "That hurt!"

"Who told you boys don't cry?"

Toby thought about it and come to think about it, nobody had. He just knew he didn't cry a lot. His male friends didn't ever cry, at least not in front of him. He remembered something from biology class at the start of the school year about girls having higher levels of prolactin, or something like that, producing more tears in girls and *why on earth was he thinking about prolactin and biology class…*

"Toby! Toby Baxter! Earth to Toby! Tears are not a sign of weakness. Tears are the Creator's way of releasing emotional stuff in our lives, whether it's happiness, sadness, or fear. You've had a big shock, Toby. You can't keep that energy inside or it will eat you up. Your tears are healing you. Tears cleanse us. Tears make us human."

Blah, blah, blah… thought Toby.

Clovor stared at him. "Did you just think 'blah, blah, blah' to yourself?"

Toby quickly looked up to see if perhaps his thoughts had written themselves above his head, but saw nothing.

"I can see it in your eyes, Toby!" she said, but her voice had become more playful.

Before he could defend himself he felt a hand on his shoulder. It was Mathilda. He looked up at her and she smiled at him. She gave him a wet towel to wipe away the tears and the snot.

"Was anyone hurt?" Toby asked.

"No," Judah said. "We didn't see any trolls. They were simply trolling us… trolling you Toby, trying to get under your skin."

"Well," Toby admitted, "it worked a charm!"

Worked a charm? Where did that come from? Toby silently wondered.

"Move away now and give Toby some air." Grandpa extended his hand to Toby and pulled him up from the beanbag chair. "Follow me, Toby."

Toby followed Grandpa down the hallway where they turned into a bedroom. The room glowed but Toby couldn't see the source of the light. The glow soothed him. The room was simple, with a single bed covered by a big fluffy blanket, a dresser, and off to the left a small bathroom. Grandma walked out of the bathroom and told Toby that she had prepared a bath for him, adding that he would find some pajamas in there along with other toiletries. Once he was done, he would find a mug of hot chocolate by his bed made with herbs to help him sleep. Grandpa and Grandma left him to it.

Toby took a long bath and tried to shut off his mind. He almost fell asleep in the tub. He got out and put on the pajamas—*Thor* pajamas! After brushing his teeth he hopped into the nice soft bed, took one sip of the hot chocolate that had magically appeared while he'd been in the bath, and then collapsed into a deep, dreamless sleep. But not before he caught a whiff of Christmas.

CHAPTER 7

The Honorary Footie Elf

Toby had no idea how long he'd slept, but apparently it was now morning. Sunlight filled the room through a window above the bed that he hadn't seen the night before. He felt surprisingly refreshed, the terror and fear of the night before an afterthought. He could still smell a hint of Christmas and it filled him with a deep sense of quiet confidence for some reason.

As he sat up he was startled to see the Healer sitting on the side of his bed.

"Good morning, Toby! How are you feeling?"

"Better. Much better. Thanks."

"We were all very concerned about you last night. I checked in on you before I went home and you were in a deep sleep. I could sense it was a healing sleep. It appears to have worked its magic. Do you feel up for some lunch? I'm afraid you slept through breakfast."

The Healer got up and headed toward the door. Before leaving he turned to Toby and asked, "Toby, do you smell pine trees and cinnamon?" The Healer asked the question as if he not only knew the answer, but knew something deeper behind the answer as well.

"Yes, sir. It's the smell of Christmas."

"Hmm." And with that, the Healer left the room, shutting the door behind him.

Toby noticed a fresh set of clothes on top of the dresser. He threw them on and, after using the bathroom, headed out into the hall for lunch. Only Grandma was there.

"Toby, honey, are you feeling better? Did you sleep well? You look stronger! The life has come back into your face. Are you hungry? Of course you are. You must be starving after yesterday. Here, sit down and I'll bring out your lunch. The rest of the gang are outside."

Toby sat down and Grandma brought him a big ham on rye sandwich. Toby wasn't a big rye bread fan but he had a hunch that this sandwich would change his mind. And it did. He was so hungry he finished off the sandwich in two minutes and then washed it down with some of that energizing elven drink.

The door to the house opened and Toby heard the sounds of people cheering. Mathilda walked in.

"Hey, sleepy head! Welcome back to the world. How was lunch? Are you ready to go out and get some fresh air?"

"Lunch was great, and sure. What's going on outside?"

"It's our weekly footie match. We're down an elf and we could use your help."

"I'm not very athletic."

"Maybe not in your world. But here… you'll be a superstar, Toby. I'm sure of it."

She led him outside. To his left and to his right he noticed small holes in the cliff wall he'd seen earlier, no doubt houses for other River Elf families. The stream ran in front of them. A bit down the stream path, to his right, was a small bridge across the stream. On the other side of the stream was a huge area of grass, with the forest curling around part of it like a half moon. Elves sat on chairs and blankets on both sides of what Toby had suspected was a ball field when he'd seen it the day before. At both ends of the field were goal posts. But not NFL type goal posts. As he and Mathilda crossed over the bridge and headed toward the field he could see that there were actually four goal posts on each end of the field. Two tall ones and two smaller ones on either side of the tall ones.

He also noticed Donold, Johanna, Ethol, and Victor standing watch at various points on the field.

He and Mathilda stood on the sideline watching the game. To his untrained eye the game made no sense at all.

The field was in the shape of an oval, not a square like American football. The players wore no gear except shorts, a sleeveless jersey, socks and shoes. The ball was shaped like an NFL football, only fatter.

But what made Toby's head spin was the game itself. It looked like each side had eighteen players. And the players were moving all the time. No huddles. No calling or setting up of plays. Just mass chaos. No quarterback or running back or cornerback. Just thirty-six people running back and forth, hitting the ball, kicking the ball, running with it for a few yards and then magically bouncing it on the ground and catching it, only to run some more, along with lots of tackling.

He watched as one person kicked the ball forward to a teammate who jumped up and caught it. For some reason, this time everyone stopped. The player with the ball pulled up his socks, held the ball in front of him, took a running start, and then kicked the ball toward the goal posts. It went straight through the two tall posts. An elf wearing what looked like a long white doctor's coat and a white, wide-brimmed hat stood between the posts and watched the ball sail over. He then stuck his two pointer fingers out and lowered his forearms from his shoulders to his hips, causing the crowd to erupt into cheers—at least the part of the crowd rooting for the team that had just scored.

"Hey, mate!" Deckor said as he ran toward Toby. "You came just in time. Our side lost one of our teammates to a slight injury."

Toby noticed a young elf writhing in pain on the sideline.

"Here," Deckor said, "put these on."

Deckor handed him a pair of spiked shoes, shorts, socks, and a jersey. Deckor then led him over to a discreet place where he could change.

"Why are you talking in a British accent?" Toby asked as he laced up his shoes.

"It's not British. It's Australian."

"Why?"

"Because the game we're playing comes from Australia, of course!"

"Of course. Makes perfect sense," said Toby, who couldn't make any sense of it at all.

He looked over his jersey. It was sleeveless with red trim and blue, yellow, and red stripes. A large blue crow took center stage on the front with the word, *Crows*, written underneath it.

He could see that the opposing team wore red jerseys with a white swan on them.

It then dawned on him that all of the clothes the elves gave to him always fit him perfectly. When he asked Deckor about it, Deckor simply smiled and said, "It must be elven magic."

"Are you magic?" asked Toby. Deckor answered only with another smile.

Toby said, "As I told Mathilda, I'm not a very good athlete."

"No worries, mate. We'll teach you on the fly. The rules are simple. The object of the game is to kick the ball through the two tall goal posts. That's worth six points and it's called a *goal*. If the ball goes between a tall post and smaller post it's called a *behind* and is worth one point… and no, it's not that kind of behind, in case you were wondering!"

"I wasn't wondering…"

"Good, mate. Now… you can't run with the ball. You can only hand pass it to your mates, the same way you might serve a volleyball, or kick it to a mate, or run with it for a few yards but then you have to bounce it occasionally or the other team gets the ball. If you kick the ball and someone catches it it's called a *mark* and you can either play on or stop, catch your breath, and kick it to another teammate. Good so far?"

"Uh…"

"You can tackle someone who's holding the ball, at which point the umpire will set up a jump ball, only not like in basketball where the ref throws the ball in the air. In this game the ref bounces the ball off of the ground. Basically, this is a mashup of rugby, basketball, volleyball, NFL, soccer, and All-Star Wrestling! Easy, right?"

"Uh…"

"Never mind. Best way to learn is to do it. Come on, it's time for the final quarter. We're losing so we could use some of that Toby Baxter magic."

"Magic? What are you talking about?" Toby asked but Deckor was already running onto the field and waving at Toby to join him.

As Toby walked onto the field something astonishing happened. The spectators on both sides of the field stood up and began cheering him: "*Toe-bee! Toe-bee! Toe-bee! Toe-bee!*"

It was perhaps the most embarrassing moment of his young life.

Deckor quickly introduced Toby to the rest of the team. Toby was glad to see that the cousins were among them. Once they'd all shaken hands, they moved to the middle of the oval for a jump ball. The ref bounced the ball off of the turf and several players from both teams moved toward it as the ball soared into the air. Judah was able to get to the ball first and batted it right into the hands of Toby, who was immediately tackled by seven elves from the opposing team. They grabbed at the ball, trying to rip it from his hands until the ref blew a whistle. They finally piled off of him and set up for another jump ball.

Once again Judah batted it into Toby hands but this time Toby quickly tried to punt it away and to his surprise, the ball traveled a fair distance into the hands of Clovor, who hand-passed it to Phoenix, who kicked it forward to one of their team members, who caught it off to the side of the oval and stopped. A long way, from Toby's perspective, from the goal.

He watched as his elven teammate pulled up his socks, looked at the goal, and then started trotting toward it. He kicked the ball and Toby was sure it would go straight into the woods, but the ball miraculously curved and went right between the two tall goal posts. The white coated-and-hatted elf moved his arms down to his hips and stuck out his two pointer fingers. Half of the crowd erupted into applause. *Goal!*

The whole team met in a circle, including Toby, and did a quick group hug before heading back to the center of the *pitch*, as he heard the elves call it.

Toby was no athlete, but on this day, in this world, he held his own. He never really knew what he was doing but the game seemed to come to him instinctively. Perhaps it was elven magic. Or Toby Baxter magic? And it didn't hurt that he was at least seven inches taller than everybody else on the field.

With forty-five seconds left and his team down by five, Toby sent a kick soaring toward the middle of the field. Clovor caught it—a *mark*—and then stopped a moment for everyone to catch up to her. Toby ran by her toward the goal area while she boomed a kick right to him. It seemed to take forever for the ball to come down. Six of the opposing team encircled him but Toby had seen something earlier and tried it. Just as the ball was coming down he jumped up, dug his knee into the back of one of the opposing players, and launched himself toward the ball, catching it in midair. He landed hard on the ground but managed to hold onto the ball.

The team rallied to him. "Take a breath Toby. You can do this. Let the time run out. Make this goal and we win the game. You can do this, mate." It was Judah. He gave Toby a pat on the back and everyone moved away to give him room.

And there stood Toby. Holding the ball. Ready to kick the game-winning goal.

He bent down and pulled up his socks. He took the measure of the goal posts... started a slow trot... building speed... and then kicked the ball with all of his might. And what a kick! It sailed high into the sky. It started out straight and strong and then at the right moment it curved toward the goal. Toby could feel his body twisting with the ball, willing it into the goal. And then... and then... it hit the goal post.

A collective "awwwwww" filled the air.

"What does that mean? What does that mean?" Toby screamed to his team members.

"Sorry, mate, it's a *behind*. One point. But great try, mate," one of the elves said as he slapped Toby on the butt.

Toby slumped to the ground utterly disappointed in himself. He'd never ever been in a game like this. His one chance to be the hero. And he blew it.

As he sat on the ground all of the players from both teams surrounded him, lifted him onto their shoulders, and carried him off the field as if he had won the game. The fans cheered his name once again as the Elves carted him to the bench.

After they set him down Toby asked Phoenix, "What was that all about?"

"They just wanted to let you know that even though you didn't get the goal, for a first timer, you played an outstanding game. Good on ya, mate!"

"Great. A participation award," Toby muttered under his breath.

Phoenix nudged Toby with his elbow. "Come on, Toby. The elves simply wanted you to know that you earned your place as an honorary footie elf today. Enjoy the moment. Now, let's get something to eat. I'm starved!"

Toby noticed that the Australian accent had disappeared… and that his elven friends really liked to eat!

CHAPTER 8

Toby Baxter Gets Some Answers—And Doesn't Like Them Very Much

After taking a quick shower Toby headed back to the hall. All of the cousins were seated around the dinner table—*how do you sit around a rectangle table?*—with Grandpa and Grandma standing nearby. It had started raining outside. Not the violent storm he'd experienced with Author, but a nice, gentle, soaking rain. The fire in the fireplace provided a sense of warmth and hominess. *Hominess? Where in the world did that word come from?*

"Toby, come and sit down," Grandpa said. "We're ready to eat."

Toby sat down, this time between Clovor and Judah. Grandpa and Grandma brought out several plates full of meats, potatoes, and vegetables, along with freshly baked bread.

"Can I help you carry something, Grandma?" Toby asked.

As Grandma shook her head no, Judah turned and whispered to him. "Grandma and Grandpa insist that they serve us our meals. They say it's their way of blessing us. Once in awhile we're able to sneak the dirty plates into the kitchen, but not often."

Toby was hungry after his big footie match. And, like the night before, the food was incredible.

While there was no dessert this time, tea was served. Toby wasn't a tea drinker. Actually, he'd never tried it. But based on his short experience in *RiverHome*, he was willing to give it a go. Not surprisingly, the tea was delicious. It tasted of oranges with a slight hint of cinnamon. And it seemed to energize his senses, making him hyper alert.

Clovor turned to him and said, "Toby, we've not had a chance to finish our story or to answer your questions. Hopefully there will be no more interruptions."

And just as she said that, there was a knock at the door. Grandpa answered it and in walked Donold, Ethol, Johanna, and Victor.

"Just in time," Clovor said.

As they were seated Clovor asked, "What would you like to know, Toby?"

Toby had lots of questions. In fact, too many questions. He didn't know where to begin.

"Um… this may seem a bit… um… well… why are you so short? Aren't elves usually taller… more my size?"

They all laughed. "We've heard the stories about tall elves… but we've never seen any… in our world, anyway," Deckor answered. "We're just the right size."

"Why do the trolls hate you?"

This time… silence.

"Why does anyone hate?" Judah broke the awkward quiet. "Think of your own world, Toby. People who hate those whose skin color is different from theirs. Nations that hate other nations and see them as their enemies. Why do they hate? A feeling of superiority? Fear? Misunderstanding? Prejudice? Jealousy? Some small grievance that turns into an obsession?"

Toby frowned. "My friend Sid has been bullied because his skin is black. Same with my friend, Bruce, because he's Jewish."

More silence.

"So again, why do the trolls hate the River Elves?" Toby asked.

"No one really knows anymore," Grandpa said. "The trolls claim that our ancestors took some of their land years long ago and then killed any troll trying to reclaim it. But we have no proof of that. Our history books say that soon after the Chaos, as the various peoples started moving away from each other, the trolls and the elves fought over the division of the resources. Those resources had been equally shared among all prior to the Chaos."

Grandpa paused for a moment. He seemed to be debating with himself what to say next. "What elves often don't talk about is our own role in the animosity. After the Chaos, perhaps we claimed a sense of superiority over the other peoples of the Earth. Perhaps the trolls felt belittled by our ancestors and their anger over that sense of shame is passed on from generation to generation. Hate is a hard animal to kill."

Toby, under the influence of his *Spidey*—or is it *Spider?*—sense enhancing tea, could feel tension around the table when Grandpa talked about the potential of the elves' role in hate.

"What do the trolls want?"

A loud slap on the table made everyone jump. It was Donold. His face was beet red and his eyes looked like they were ready to explode out of his head.

"WHO CARES!" he yelled. "What does it matter? Those trolls killed my parents. They killed your parents, Clovor, Phoenix, and Deckor. And yours, Judah and Mathilda. They hate us. They want to destroy us. It's time to stop talking about them and finally face them in battle. If they want a fight, let's fight! That's why the Hero is here, isn't it?"

The room fell silent once again. Toby looked around the table. Every head was bowed except for Grandma's and Donold's. Grandma got up, walked over to Donold, and put her arms around him. Donold tried to push her away but she was tough and held him until he gave up. For what felt like several minutes Grandma seemed to absorb Donold's anger and pain.

Another knock on the door brought everyone back into the moment. It was the Healer. He pulled up a chair to the table and looked around from face to face. The Healer could sense something had happened but he said nothing.

"Have you tried negotiating with the trolls?" Toby knew immediately that was the wrong question to ask.

Once again Donold exploded. "Twenty-five of your years ago we sent two of our best leaders to negotiate a peace and they never returned. The trolls responded by attacking us, leading to the Troll War. YOU CANNOT NEGOTIATE WITH THEM!" Donold was shouting again. This time Toby could see on the faces of those around the table that the anger ran deep in all of them, not just in Donold. They all sat quietly in their grief.

"Tell me about the Sword in the stone by the waterfall."

"The Sword is somewhat of a mystery, Toby." Phoenix was the one to answer. "The Sword has been there... *had* been there... for thousands of years. Somehow it stands guard over us. Whenever a crisis threatens *RiverHome*, the Sword seemingly comes to life, announcing the name of the Hero who will wield it along side of us."

Toby stared at him. And then he stared at each of the faces around the table staring back at him.

"I know you said this last night. But you're serious? You think I'm the Hero?"

"No, Toby Baxter, the Sword called you. The Sword declared you our Hero," Phoenix answered.

"I don't understand. I'm a thirteen-year-old kid, and just barely thirteen. I don't have any magic powers."

"It's true," Mathilda interrupted. "He's no Harry Potter!" She giggled. But a quick look from Judah wiped the smile from her face.

"She's right. I'm no Harry Potter. I'm no Percy Jackman…"

"I think he means Percy Jackson," Mathilda added helpfully, "or Hugh Jackman, who played the Wolverine in the movies…" Another sharp look from Judah.

"Whatever his name is, I'm not like him. I don't have any super powers to help you with. If anything, I'm more like the World's Wimpiest Kid!"

"Toby," Grandma said. "The Sword chose you for a reason. The Sword brought you here to help us. To help with what, we still don't know… yet. And what that help will look like, we have no idea. What we do know is that the trolls have been moving closer and closer to *RiverHome*. Their power seems to be growing as evidenced by how they were able to smash the Sword's monument and take the Sword. And what we also know is that, whether you realize it or not, you do have the superpowers we need, or the Sword would not have called you."

"About that," Toby said. "If the trolls have the Sword, what good am I to you now? And why don't they simply use the Sword against you? Against us?"

"Only you can wield the Sword, Toby," Grandma answered. "Their only hope is to keep it from you."

"That still doesn't answer my question about not having any super or magical powers. I have nothing to offer you."

"Toby," Grandpa said, "you were created with superpowers. In your world you call them abilities or talents or skills or gifts. But they look like magical powers when you use them. You just don't know what they are yet."

"Yeah! Like today. Have you ever played footie before?" Phoenix asked.

"Uh, no..." Toby said hesitantly.

"And you told Deckor and Mathilda that you're not a very good athlete, right? But look at how well you did playing footie today. Watching you learn the game as quickly as you did was magical!"

"It was the elven juice you gave me. It was the magic of this land. It was dumb luck. But it wasn't a superpower."

"Toby Baxter," Clovor said, her eyes drilling into his. "You and you alone, with no help from us, played footie like a champion today. Today you discovered a skill, a talent, a superpower."

Everyone around the table looked at him until he began to squirm.

"I'm scared. I'm terrified. I'm just a kid. I can't do this."

Just as Mathilda was about to say something the Healer stood up. "Toby Baxter, tell them what we smelled in your room today."

They all looked at the Healer and then at Toby.

"We smelled Christmas."

Every single person around the table inhaled. The room went silent.

"You... you... you smelled Christmas?" Mathilda asked.

Toby looked at all of them wondering what the big deal was. "Yes, I smelled Christmas in my room this morning, but it wasn't the first time."

"Wait! What?" Deckor asked.

"I smelled it around the time you came to see me, Deckor. The first time was after I saw you at my school. I went home and a big giant stood in front of my bedroom window."

Phoenix looked like he was about to faint. "You saw the Giant?"

"Twice! He showed up again at my birthday party right after Deckor disappeared."

Everyone looked at Deckor.

"I didn't see him. Honest!" Deckor said.

"What does he look like?" the Healer asked.

"Don't you know?"

"No," the Healer answered. "No one has ever seen him before. We only have the ancient stories about him."

"He's big. About nine feet tall. He has a trimmed brown beard, and long brown hair with some grey in it. He wears a wreath on his head and a green robe with a white collar. And he has big green eyes."

"That's the Christmas Elf, alright!" Phoenix said, almost jumping out of his chair.

"Elf? He's a giant!"

"Yes, but we refer to him as the Christmas Elf. Don't some of your stories refer to Santa as an elf? We like to think he's a distant relative along with the elves who make all of those Christmas gifts. By the way those elves are the same size as we are. Anyway, while he doesn't have an official name, I call him Barry. Get it? Barry Christmas? No? How about Larry Christmas? Terry Christmas? Harry Christmas?" Phoenix finally ran out of breath.

"Why is this Giant important to you?" Toby asked.

"Toby," the Healer said. "Tell us again what you smell when the Christmas Elf is near you."

"Christmas. At least the smells I think of when I think about Christmas. Pine trees. Cinnamon. Maybe sugar cookies."

"What else?"

"I'm not sure what you're asking."

"What else do you smell, not with your nose, but with your heart?"

Toby thought about that question for several seconds. "Calm. Peace. Safety. Is that what you're getting at?"

"Go deeper, Toby Baxter. What's behind the calm, peace, and safety?"

Toby had no idea what the Healer was getting at. But everyone else around the table seemed to know the answer. And then it hit him.

"Hope! I smell hope!"

"Toby Baxter," the Healer said as he walked over and laid his hands on Toby's shoulders, "you have not only been chosen by the Sword to be our Hero, but you have been blessed by the Creator with the greatest super hero power of them all. The Quest ahead of you will be filled with danger, fear, and even terror. You will lose heart when the task you are called to do becomes impossible. And in that moment somehow, in someway, the Christmas Elf will be there to give you hope. Hope, Toby Baxter, will find you when you are lost in despair. Hope, Toby Baxter, will get you through."

"Quest? Danger? Fear? Terror? Lost? Despair?" Toby could barely get the words out.

"And Hope, Toby Baxter! Hope!"

Everyone stared at Toby as he tried to process everything he'd just heard. He wondered when he was going to wake up.

Grandpa walked over and helped Toby out of his chair. "Come with me, son. That's enough for today." Grandpa led him to the bedroom and helped Toby into his *Thor* pajamas. He skipped the teeth brushing. Instead, Toby crawled into bed numb, scared—terrified was more like it—and exhausted. Grandpa sat on the edge of the bed and began to hum a deep, low, Celtic melody that somehow soothed Toby and calmed his anxiety. He fell asleep, but this time it was anything but a dreamless sleep.

CHAPTER 9

About that Quest

Toby was back in his closet. It was pitch dark but he had found the door. He turned the door handle only to find it locked. He started banging on the door, getting more desperate with each passing minute. "Dad! Mom! Dad! Mom! Get me out of here! Get me out of here!"

Toby opened his eyes. He looked around. He was in his elven bed in his elven room. Someone was banging on his door.

"Toby! Toby! Are you all right? Can I come in?" It was Clovor.

Toby sat up and rubbed his eyes. "Yes. Come on in."

Clovor tentatively walked into his room and sat down on the side of his bed. "You were calling for your dad and mom. Were you having a nightmare?"

"Must have been."

"Will you be OK?"

Toby sat for a moment and then nodded yes. "Sorry, I'm trying to get my bearings and wake up."

"Are you hungry? Grandma has outdone herself today with waffles, whipped cream, strawberries, and fried eggs. Oh, and some bacon."

That got his attention. "Bacon! I'm in. Let me get dressed. I'll be out in five minutes."

Before he could get out of bed, however, Mathilda stuck her head into the room. "Hey, Harry Potter. Did you sleep well?"

"Ha! Ha! Ha! Good morning to you, too, Hermione."

"Toby's just about to get up and join us for breakfast," Clovor said. "He'd had a nightmare."

"I heard it in my room down the hall," Mathilda said. "But not to worry. Grandma's waffles will help you feel a whole lot better."

Toby threw on his elven leathers and headed into the hall. The cousins were there, along with Grandpa and Grandma. All of them had that "are you OK?" look on their faces. He smiled at them and sat down between Mathilda and Phoenix.

Grandpa prayed over the meal and he, along with Grandma, served the breakfast. It was better than advertised. These elves sure loved their meals. Toby ate until his stomach refused to accept another bite.

"Hey, Toby, while the rest of them clean up the plates, let's go for a walk." Clovor grabbed a light jacket as they headed out the door. Toby looked at Phoenix and mouthed, "You're going to clear the table?" Phoenix grinned.

It was a beautiful, fresh morning. The rain from the night before had seemingly cleaned everything up. Toby noticed footie being played on the pitch on the other side of the stream. "How is it, with the trolls threatening you, that you're still able to play games? Shouldn't you all be on high alert?"

"We are on high alert, Toby. You just don't see it. But we have to live our lives as well. Let's head this way."

"Hey, wait for me," Mathilda yelled as she ran after them.

The three of them followed the stream in the opposite direction of the waterfall for about a mile. The path led them through a light forest with high rock walls on either side of the stream. Occasionally they had to wade through the stream to the other side and then back again, but the water was never too deep, and Clovor and Mathilda knew where they were going.

They didn't speak as they made their way down the stream. The stream led them out of the forest onto the banks of a big, rushing river. Toby looked to his left and was able to see the river for about a city block or so before it curved out of sight. To his right the river changed course about eight city blocks downstream. The roar of the river along with the sound of the birds singing in the trees behind them brought a deep sense of calm to him.

"This is the *River Glaedaan*. Our ancestors have lived near this river for centuries. It serves as a border of sorts from the trolls. But as you've seen, not a very secure border these days. The trolls live on the other side of the river, through that forest, about a hundred miles from here."

"So how do you protect your border?"

Mathilda pointed up and behind them. Toby saw what looked like houses high in the trees. In each of the boxes or houses was an elf. Some of them waved at him. Others kept their eyes glued to the river.

The three of them sat down on a grassy area overlooking the river.

"How close are the trolls to us right now?"

"Don't worry, Toby. As of this moment we're safe. The trolls, with the exception of a few scouts, are back in their village," Clovor explained.

"Are the troll scouts the ones who gave you your injuries a few days ago? Just as I was arriving?"

It was Mathilda who answered. "We had a very small skirmish right over there." She pointed to her left. "We got in a few blows of our own before the trolls ran off down the river, to where I assume their boats were waiting for them. Thankfully they didn't mean to kill us—this time! It was a warning. They were trying to scare us. But it didn't work. It only hurt a bit!"

"If the trolls are a hundred miles away from here, how is it that we can hear that awful, terrifying scream?"

Both Clovor and Mathilda stared off into the river. "We're not sure how they do it, to be honest. Somehow they are able to amplify their battle cry across the miles. And you're right. It is terrifying," Clovor agreed.

"Battle cry?"

"Perhaps you learned about the Rebel Yell at school. During your Civil War the Rebels would run into the battlefield with a cry that some said sounded like a rabbit screaming. Apparently, it was described as a sound so frightening that it created a corkscrew-like sensation up and down the spine. To be gruesome, it turned the insides of bowels to liquid, if you know what I mean. The Scottish in your world used something similar to fill their enemies with terror. That's what the trolls are doing."

"How do you know about our history?"

"Sadly," Clovor answered, "we've had to become students of warfare."

Toby sensed from her body language that Clovor took no joy in war or violence.

"This last time that scream or battle cry or whatever… I heard words. It was more than a scream. It was a warning," he said.

"We heard it, too," said Mathilda. She just shook her head.

"You said that whenever the elves are in trouble the Sword calls a Hero. Did the Sword call a Hero to fight with you during…"

Without warning an arrow flew within inches of Toby's ear, embedding itself in the tree behind him. More arrows hissed by as Clovor and Mathilda threw themselves on top of him. After a few moments they dragged him to his feet, grabbed him by his arms, and at the same time yelled "RUN!"

Toby didn't need any convincing. He took off as fast as he could with Clovor and Mathilda running behind him as a shield. He could hear the elves in the trees shouting orders to each other.

TOBY BAXTER!

The horrific battle cry.

THAT WAS YOUR FINAL WARNING. GO HOME. YOU CANNOT HELP THE ELVES. GO HOME!

And then the shrieking stopped. Toby, along with Clovor and Mathilda, had run most of the way back to the village but stopped when the battle cry stopped. Phoenix, Judah, and Deckor, were running toward them with swords and daggers drawn.

"Are you OK? Where are they? Was anyone hurt?" The questions tumbled out of Judah.

"We're… OK. It was… just… a warning," Clovor said, bent over trying to catch her breath. "Not sure… how…they got past… our guards… again!"

"Toby, are you all right?" Deckor asked.

Toby didn't answer. He stared at each of them one by one. His face was red, but not from running.

Toby Baxter was furious.

"About that Quest," he said, trying to catch his breath. "When do we start?"

As they headed back to the house, Toby heard the voice of his grandfather: "*How will you use your power?*"

CHAPTER 10

The Drone

Toby could hear Donold yelling before they got into the house.

"HOW DID THOSE TROLLS GET PAST OUR SECURITY? DID ANYONE SEE THEM? WHERE DID THEY COME FROM?" He hit the table a few times to add effect.

Toby noticed what he took to be two River Elf Security Patrols. They were dressed in the same type of elven leather as Toby and the others, but the colors were more camouflaged. Each also wore a dark green sash from his right shoulder to his left hip. As was true with the other elves, he couldn't tell their ages, but he assumed they were younger recruits. And while they took the full force of Donold's outrage like pros, Toby could see the fear in their eyes. He guessed they'd probably rather be in hand-to-hand combat with trolls than facing the wrath of Donold.

Donold's questions were met with silence. Apparently, no one saw anything and had no idea where the volley of arrows had come from. The Patrols were dismissed.

They walked past Toby, saluting him by tapping the left side of their chests with their right fists. As they did so one of them whispered to the other, "He looks like his dad."

"Wait! What?" Toby said. "What did you say about my dad?"

But as he turned to go after the Patrols... he heard it.

"*Squaaawk! Toby Baxter! Squaaawk!*"

Toby jumped and at the same time moved backwards, tripping over his feet and falling to the floor. He looked up toward the sound and saw the biggest *crow?... raven?... magpie?—what does a magpie look like and do I even know what a magpie is and how had that come into my mind?*—he'd ever seen. It was the size of a chubby beagle.

Toby tried scooting away from it, unable to take his eyes off of it. Moments later he wished he had taken his eyes off of it. He watched in revulsion as the bird shook its head and its head morphed into a... human head! The head was covered with blue-black feathers. The eyebrows were blue-black feathers. Its goatee... *a goatee?...* was made of feathers. It still had a bird body, but now had a human neck and a human head.

That wasn't the end of the shock. When the now human-headed bird spoke, it did so in a deep, polite manner. And no mistaking it this time. This, whatever it was, had an English accent.

"Toby Baxter, my good fellow. It is a pleasure to make your acquaintance."

Toby looked around at the elves, hoping to find someone as shocked as he was. But they all stood around him, seeming to enjoy his confusion and discomfort.

Finally, Phoenix offered him his hand and pulled Toby to his feet.

Donold stepped forward. "Toby Baxter, this is Hiriam. Hiriam is a Drone. He works with us."

"A drone?"

"Yes, a Drone. He does surveillance for us. The River Elves and the Drones have been friends for centuries."

With the introduction out of the way Donold turned to Hiriam. "Did you see anything? Did any of the other Drones see anything? How did those trolls break through our security?"

"I'm sorry to report, my good friend, that neither I, nor my fellow Drones, saw anything. We were just as surprised as you. But I will tell you this. There were no trolls in the area prior to the attack. In fact, I can guarantee it. There is nothing to indicate the presence of trolls with the exception of the arrows."

"Are you saying the trolls didn't fire the arrows? Or that somehow they were able to launch those arrows from beyond our security zone? Or that they were able to sneak in under our noses?" Clovor sounded concerned.

"I cannot say for sure, Friend Clovor. But we will do our best to get answers for you."

Then Hiriam the Drone turned to Toby.

"Toby Baxter. You have been brought here for such a time as this. It is an honor, Friend, to fight in this noblest of causes with you."

Toby knew he had just agreed to join the River Elves in their Quest against the trolls. But the mention of fighting brought him back down to earth, or at least back down to *RiverHome*.

"Thank you, Hiriam," was all he could mutter.

"Hiriam will be our point person on behalf of the Drones in our Quest, Toby. The Drones will help guide us on the safest route possible," Donold said.

"You can count on us, Good Fellow Donold, but as you know, there are no safe routes into the land of the trolls."

"We're going into troll land?" Toby asked with no small amount of fear in his voice.

Mathilda playfully punched his arm. "Where did you think our Quest would take us, Toby? Disneyland?"

"Ha. Ha. Ha. Tinker Bell." Toby tried his best to put confidence into his voice.

Clovor said, "We will plan out the Quest this evening after dinner. In the meantime, I managed to grab a few arrows. Phoenix and Judah, can you please examine them to make sure they are troll arrows?"

"What are you thinking?" Deckor asked.

"I don't know what I'm thinking so I won't think it until I have more information."

"Good, sage advice, Madame Clovor. If I may be excused, I will go and dine with my fellow Drones and come back in a few hours to join you in the planning of the Quest. Until then, peace and safety, Friends of the Drones."

With that Hiriam shook his human head, turning it back into a bird head. He opened his massive wings, jumped, and soared out of the hall and presumably into the sky outside.

"*Squaaawk I'll be back! Squaaawk!*"

"Come,' Grandpa said. "Your baths are waiting. Dinner will be served in forty-five minutes."

Toby didn't need to be told twice. A nice, warm River Elf bath was just the thing a frightened thirteen-year-old, about to embark on a life-or-death Quest, needed.

CHAPTER 11

Betrayal

After the table had been cleared of the dinner dishes, Donold laid out a large map onto it. Toby took a quick look. He saw the waterfall and presumably the hole leading back to his bedroom. He saw the stream and the forested area and the footie pitch on the other side. He saw the path leading to the *River Glaedaan*. Something about the map looked familiar. Then he gasped.

"What is it, Toby?" asked Donold.

"This map..."

"What about it?"

"I've seen it before. My dad gave me a small copy of it a few days before my birthday. How is that possible?"

But that was as far as the conversation got, because at that moment the door opened and the rest of the High Council entered the hall.

Everyone took a seat without speaking. It was apparent to Toby that this was going to be a tense meeting.

Suddenly everyone stood up. As they did so, Grandpa walked in wearing a long scabbard at his side and a large shiny medallion around his neck.

"Commander!" Donold said. They all saluted Grandpa, bringing their right fists to the left of their chests.

Commander? thought Toby.

Grandpa nodded at them and everyone took their seats once again.

Grandpa spoke. "My son, Mikol—your father, Clovor, Phoenix, and Deckor—asked me to let him lead our soldiers into battle against the trolls after the trolls killed our diplomats. I hesitated, but I knew that it was time to let him take command. Mikol and his wife, Ambor, along with Coron and Alyeon, your parents," he nodded to Judah and Mathilda, "fought bravely alongside our Elven warriors. But they lost their lives."

The room fell silent as they remembered their loss and grief.

"Clovor, I know that you believe it is now your time to lead our people on this Quest. I am once again hesitant because I cannot bear the thought of losing you, your siblings, your cousins, or any of those who will embark on this mission with you."

Grandpa looked directly at Toby and Toby felt the hairs on the back of his neck stand up.

"But I have no taste for blood, war, or violence. I do not have the energy required for this Quest. And so, Clovor, please rise."

Clovor stood up and walked over to Grandpa, then fell to one knee. Grandpa drew the sword from his scabbard and touching both of her shoulders with it said to her, "Clovor, go in the strength of *RiverHome*, the River Elves, and our Creator. Lead with honor and valor, my dear Grandchild. And..." Grandpa choked up. "Come home!"

As Clovor stood up the High Council stood as well. Grandpa removed his medallion, at which point Toby noticed an image of the Sword in the stone engraved on it, and placed it around Clovor's neck.

Grandpa hugged Clovor, turned, and walked out of the room. Clovor returned to her seat and as she sat, the High Council sat.

"Donold, you will, of course, continue on as our Chief Strategist and Captain."

Donold nodded his head in acknowledgment.

"Toby," Clovor said as she turned her attention to him. "Normally when the Sword summons a Hero we know what the crisis is. We knew, for example, twenty-five of your years ago, that we needed a Hero to help us in our battle against the trolls."

"If I may, Commander?" Toby had a question. "The River Elves lost that battle, didn't they? Did the Hero fail? Did the Hero not come in time?"

"Toby, for now what you need to know—and need to remember—is that the Hero came at the right time. *RiverHome* is here today because the Hero saved us. The rest of the story must wait until we get back home… if we get back home."

"Not so crazy about that 'if!'" Toby muttered to himself.

Squaaawk! Squaaawk! Squaawk!

Hiriam flew into the room and took his place on a large stand apparently created for him. Toby had been so surprised by the Drone earlier that he hadn't seen the Drone's chair, so to speak, near the table. The Drone shook his bird head, revealing his human head, making Toby gag a bit.

"Friends, I apologize for the lateness of my arrival. But I'm afraid I bear some rather disturbing news."

Hiriam noticed the medallion around Clovor's neck and bowed to her slightly.

"Commander, one of our Drones is missing. When we went to check his nest, we found this. He must have left in a hurry or surely he would have gotten rid of it."

Hiriam dropped a small scroll onto the table that had been tucked under his wing.

Everyone gasped.

After several moments of silence Clovor saw the confusion on Toby's face. "Toby, that scroll is made of troll papyrus. We would recognize it anywhere. Did you read it, Hiriam?"

"Yes, Commander. It doesn't say much but it bears the seal of Clygon."

Another gasp.

"Clygon is the Tribal Chief of the trolls, Toby," whispered Mathilda.

"Who is the missing Drone?" Clovor asked Hiriam.

"Demetrius. My second in command."

The Elves stared at Hiriam, trying to take the news.

Judah chimed in. "We examined the arrows and yes, they are troll arrows. Demetrius must have been helping them all along."

Donold shook his head. "He knows everything about us! When I get my hands on him…"

"So, Hiriam, you think that Demetrius has been a spy for the trolls." Clovor interrupted. It was more of a statement than a question. "It would certainly explain a lot, like how trolls were able to sneak in and out of *RiverHome* to steal the Sword in the stone. And how they attacked us the day Toby arrived. And how trolls were able to get past our sentinels and fire arrows at us today. Demetrius knows the hidden paths in and out of *RiverHome*…"

Clovor paused.

"But why…?" She left the question hanging in the air.

Mathilda picked it up. "But why, if they knew all of the secret ways in and out of here, did they not just launch a surprise attack on us? We were sitting ducks the whole time. They had us. Why didn't they attack?"

Everyone turned their attention to Clovor.

"You suspect something, don't you, Clovor." Phoenix said.

After several moments she said quietly, looking at Toby, "Clygon has been provoking us. He has orchestrated this whole thing. He doesn't simply want to defeat us. Clygon wants the Hero. He's forcing our hand… to get us to bring the Hero to him!"

Everyone turned their attention to Toby. Toby felt the room closing in on him, his panic starting to rise.

"Then change of plans!" Deckor shouted. "There's no way we're leading Toby into that trap!"

At that, everyone started talking at once. As the discussion grew louder and more intense, Toby's head started to spin.

After several minutes of arguing, Clovor stood up. The room fell silent.

"Toby. The Sword called you here. This is your Quest. Only you can decide what we do next."

Toby swallowed. He felt the sweat running down his neck.

"I have to go, right? I'm the only one who can use the Sword? If what you have been saying is true, we have to get that Sword in my hands or at least get my hands on that Sword. Although, I still have no idea how that will make any difference."

"Toby's right," Judah said. "The Sword always and only calls the Hero when necessary. Usually, we know the reason why. But this time… admittedly," Judah scratched his head, "we're in the dark."

"Judah! Yes! Thank you!" Clovor said. "The Sword always and only calls the Hero when necessary. So, while we don't yet know the exact nature of Toby's Quest, we do know that the Sword called him here for this moment. Clygon thinks he's laying a trap for us. But the Sword will lead us as it has always done."

Clovor looked again at Toby. "And, Toby," she said, "we will be there with you. All of the resources of *RiverHome* are at your disposal."

Toby's head ached.

"Commander," Hiriam said softly. "Before you proceed. If I may. This happened on my watch. I am ashamed, and hereby resign my position as head Drone."

"No!" Clovor almost shouted at him. "No, Hiriam. I trust you with my life. Demetrius made his own decision. This is not on you. I will hear no more of him or of your shame."

Clovor sat back down.

"Phoenix, Deckor, Judah, Mathilda, Donold, and Johanna will travel with you, Toby, as will I and the Healer. It will be our job to protect you wherever the Quest may lead you. You will not have the benefit of the Sword to protect you on this Quest, as it protected previous Heroes. Hiriam and two of his most trusted Drones… and make sure you can trust them, Hiriam!… will lead us and protect us from the sky."

Ouch! Toby thought, *so Clovor is not as forgiving as she says.* But then he saw her wink at Hiriam, who bowed his head in acknowledgement.

"Victor, Ethol, you will stay and act on my behalf to protect *RiverHome* at all costs. Grandpa will serve as my second in command from here." Victor and Ethol bowed their heads slightly.

"Now that Demetrius knows we're on to him, his spies will have headed back to Clygon," Donold said. "That should clear the way for us tomorrow, but we'll need to stay sharp and alert."

"Good. Thank you, Donold. Hiriam, do you have anything else to report?" Clovor asked.

Toby took in very little of the discussion after that. His mind was numb with what he had just heard. He was about to embark on a Quest to who knows where, walking into a trap to find a Sword that was supposed to be safe in *RiverHome* but had been stolen by trolls, and he had no apparent ability to protect himself. He felt powerless. He felt thirteen!

"Toby… Toby… Toby!" He jerked back to the moment and noticed everyone staring at him. "Toby," Clovor said, "we must leave tomorrow.

You will need to get as much sleep as possible. We have a hard journey ahead of us to an uncertain destination. Follow Donold and he will get you ready for the Quest."

And with that the High Council, following the lead of Clovor, rose from their chairs and set about the business of getting ready to head into the land of the trolls.

"Awesome!" Toby muttered sarcastically under his breath as he followed Donold down the hallway to the room at the end.

CHAPTER 12

You Wouldn't Happen to Have a Slingshot and Five Stones?

At the end of the hallway stood a large door. Donold opened it and asked Toby to enter ahead of him. The room—more accurately, another hall—almost took his breath away. Like the other elven rooms, it glowed and again he had no clue as to the source of the light. Though he'd never been in such a room Toby knew immediately that it was the Armory because—*Duh!*—it was filled with all kinds of weapons: swords, arrows, axes, daggers, shields, quivers, and what appeared to be armor.

"Here, try this on." Donold threw Toby a piece of chain mail. Toby expected it to bowl him over but it was fairly light. He put it on and it fit quite nicely. *Quite nicely?* Toby asked himself. *This is armor, not a pair of underwear!*

"Now, try this." Donold handed him a sword. Toby lifted it up but it was too heavy and clumsy. And besides, he didn't have a clue as to how to use it.

"You wouldn't happen to have a slingshot and five stones, would you?"

Donold stared at him.

"Never mind. It's from a story I heard in church.

"Look, Donold, I have no idea how to wield a sword. Is that the right word? Wield? And I can't shoot arrows..."

Donold grunted. "Doesn't matter. Clovor—Commander Clovor—insists that I give you something so that you can pretend to defend yourself. Try this."

It was a light-weight dagger. It seemed to fit Toby's grip and the belt—*is it called a Scabbard?*—when pulled tight enough, at least stayed up around his skinny hips.

"That will have to do," Donold said. "Time for bed."

"Um… Donold. Could I ask you a question?"

"No."

"I'm confused about the Troll War. You all talk about defeat and how the elves lost. And yet apparently the Hero saved you. I have the feeling that I'm not getting the whole story."

"It's for Clovor to tell," Donold responded. Then his face softened. "It was a defeat for us because we lost people we loved. And the war didn't stop our conflict with the trolls. At the same time the Hero saved us from total defeat—he saved us to fight another day. We are obviously still here and have been fairly safe from the trolls for the last twenty-five of your years. That's the way of it with war. No one really wins. What you need to know right now is what Commander Clovor told you: The Hero did not let us down. Don't forget that!" Donold led him out of the armory to his bedroom.

"Goodnight, Toby Baxter. Enjoy your last night's sleep in a real bed." Then Donold's face lit up with a big smile and Toby could hear him laughing as he disappeared off down the hallway.

Toby got himself ready for bed, and just as he was about to lie down—*or was he about to lay down?*—he heard a knock at the door. It was the Healer.

"I thought you might want something to help you sleep tonight."

"What is it?" Toby asked.

"It's an elven mixture of herbs from along the stream. It has a pleasant enough taste to it and it really works."

Toby sat quietly, holding the mug the Healer had handed him.

"You're nervous?"

"Terrified is the better word," Toby replied.

"Good! That means you're ready." With that the Healer left the room, shutting the door behind him.

Toby drank the sleep aid in one gulp. The Healer was right. It did have a pleasant taste. He laid down on his pillow—*or did he lie down on his pillow?*—his mind whirling with what was about to happen in a few hours.

He was sure that there was no way he would fall asle…

CHAPTER 13

Couldn't We Take a Bus?

Toby woke up slowly and gently. He hadn't felt this rested since he had arrived in *RiverHome*. He needed to get some of that sleep stuff and take it home with him. If he ever got back home. He could tell from the window that it was still dark outside. Apparently, he hadn't slept long, but he had slept deeply.

He heard a gentle knocking on the door. It was Judah.

"Toby, breakfast is ready. We leave in an hour."

"What time is it?"

"Three a.m. We want to get as far as we can while it's still dark."

Toby threw on his elven leathers and headed to the breakfast hall. Grandpa and Grandma had outdone themselves this time; eggs, sausage, toast, pancakes, fresh fruit, and fresh-squeezed orange juice. As Toby ate it felt like a last meal. *Is it?* he wondered. Everyone around the table ate in silence.

After breakfast Toby went back to his room to get ready. Sitting outside of his door was a huge backpack. He assumed it was for him to carry. The backpack looked like it weighed at least fifty pounds. He rummaged inside it and found rain gear, dry foods, and a small shovel—*a small shovel?*

For what?—among other things. When he picked up the pack it felt more like ten pounds. *How do they do that?*

After using the bathroom—was this the last time he'd have an actual toilet and toilet paper?... *wait a minute, how am I supposed to go to the bathroom out in the wild?... is that what the small shovel is for?... gross!*—he "suited up." He put his new chainmail over his tunic and attached the dagger to his side. Then he threw the backpack over his shoulder and headed out of his nice, comfy, safe bedroom for the last time. Part of him wished he could take a selfie to remember the moment.

He was the last one to the hall. They were waiting for him. And when they saw him, they all burst out laughing. He had no idea what was so funny. He looked around and saw nothing out of the ordinary. Maybe... hopefully... they were laughing because it had all been a joke and there would be no Quest.

Grandpa walked over to him and whispered, "Your chain mail is on backwards and your dagger is hanging upside down." He helped Toby get everything on correctly. At least he didn't have toilet paper hanging out the back of his pants! He was thankful he hadn't taken that selfie.

Mathilda walked over and punched him playfully on the arm. "Don't worry, Toby! We'll get you through this!"

"You'd better!" he muttered.

The group formed a circle and joined hands. Toby stood between Deckor and Judah. He was embarrassed that his hands were sweaty but neither of the elves noticed, or were too kind to say anything.

Grandpa stood in the middle of the circle, both hands raised in the air. As he spoke, he turned so that he could address each person face to face.

"Go in peace. Go in strength. Go in the power and grace of the Creator."

As the circle broke and the group threw on their weapons and backpacks, Grandpa pulled Toby aside. He asked Toby to kneel.

As Toby did so Grandpa placed his left hand on Toby's right shoulder, and his right hand on the top of Toby's head. Even though he was kneeling Toby was still almost eye-to-eye with Grandpa.

As Grandpa looked into his eyes, Toby could feel Grandpa's power. It was if Grandpa were willing his masculine energy into him.

"Toby, you are now one of us. Show yourself to be an elf! Show yourself to be a man! I am proud of you, son."

Even though Toby knew he was only thirteen, Grandpa's words filled him with a sense of determination to live up to Grandpa's command.

By now the Quest group had encircled Grandpa and Toby.

Grandpa pulled a small vile out from his tunic. After putting on lightweight gloves, he opened the vile, poured a dark green liquid onto his thumb, and took hold of Toby's right hand. He traced a green line from the top of Toby's wrist to the knuckle of his middle finger. For a moment the liquid burned, almost like acid. Toby tried to pull his hand away but Grandpa held it firm.

"Toby, today I'm marking you as a reminder that you are not alone. We are with you. Your Creator is with you. Hope is with you. Whenever you feel alone, look at this mark and remember."

Then Grandpa pulled Toby close and whispered into his ear: "Bring my grandchildren back to us, Toby Baxter. Bring them all back home to us."

Toby had no idea what to say. "I will," he promised feebly.

As Toby turned to join the group, Grandpa whispered, "Just a minute, Toby. I have something else for you."

Grandpa walked down the hallway to his bedroom and came back moments later holding something in his hand.

"This will guide you, Toby, as you face the greatest challenges of your young life."

Grandpa handed him a compass. An ancient looking compass. The same compass that had been hand drawn on the back of the map Toby's dad had given to him at *Dairy Queen!* The same H-E-R-O as the coordinates.

"I've seen this compass before. It was on a card my dad gave me." Toby shook his head, confused as to how this could be possible.

Toby stared at the compass, wondering how exactly it would help him face whatever Grandpa was talking about, when Clovor interrupted him.

"It's time to go, Toby."

Toby put the compass into his pocket, bowed to Grandpa, and joined the group.

They headed out the door: Clovor, Phoenix, Deckor, Judah, Mathilda, Donold, Johanna, the Healer, and Toby Baxter. It was pitch dark outside. If it weren't for the torches Donold, Johanna, and Judah carried, he wouldn't have been able to see a thing.

Mathilda walked on one side of him, Deckor on the other.

"How far are we going?" Toby asked.

"Far." That was all Deckor offered. He didn't seem to be in a chatty mood. Who could blame him?

"Hiriam's intel suggests that we have to travel about eighty to eighty-five miles to get to the outskirts of the main troll stronghold," Mathilda offered.

"Hold on. Eighty-five miles? Are we walking the whole way?" Toby asked.

"Of course, Toby. How else would we get there?"

"Mules? Horses? A camper van? A bus perhaps?"

"We've never really taken to horses, Toby. We prefer to be on the ground, on our feet, ready to move and act on a moment's notice."

"But eighty-five miles! I don't think I've walked more than a mile at one time in my life. I'm always riding my bike or riding in a car or flying on an airplane. There's no way my feet are in that kind of walking shape."

"Trust the shoes, Toby." Mathilda giggled as she said it.

Toby looked down at the hairy boots given to him for this Quest. When he had first met the River Elves he had mistaken the boots for hobbit feet. He willed them to keep his feet comfy and blister-free for the journey.

By now they had arrived at the *River Glaedaan*. Toby could hear it more than see it.

"Can you swim, Toby?" Deckor asked.

"Across that river?" Toby responded in fear. "Are you kidding me?"

"Yes, he is, Toby. We're taking a raft across." Mathilda reached up and put her hand on his shoulder to calm him down. He could sense she was giving Deckor the stink eye, but who could tell? It was still too dark to even make out faces unless the torchlight was on them.

Deckor and Mathilda helped Toby onto the raft. Quietly and slowly the group made their way across the *River Glaedaan*. Donold and Johanna used long sticks to guide the raft but the river current was strong, taking them downstream. No one seemed to panic.

The trip across the river took about thirty minutes and landed them a mile or so downstream. They climbed off the raft and walked up a small hill, where Toby could just make out the outlines of a forest. It was then that the orange juice decided it was time to leave his system. And the eggs. And the pancakes. This was going to be embarrassing.

Apparently, however, others had the same urge, so to speak. The men headed off to the right and the women to the left.

"Um..." whispered Toby to Deckor. "I've never done... um... this before... outside of a bathroom. How do I not get... um... you know... all over myself?"

Deckor let out the loudest laugh Toby had ever heard. He had the sense that Deckor was actually crying, he was laughing so hard.

Once he regained his composure, Deckor said, "Do you want me to show you… or tell you?" and then he laughed some more.

After a brief tutorial Toby headed over to what he hoped would be a private, bug-free area, and answered the call of nature. To his great delight he found hand wipes in his backpack that also served a more useful purpose. *Better than toilet paper!* he thought. He then grabbed his small shovel and covered over the gift he had left the forest.

As he rejoined the group, he overheard Deckor telling the guys about Toby's dilemma. They all had a good laugh.

But Toby felt weirdly proud of himself. If he ever got lost in a forest back home he'd at least know how to go to the bathroom! Not that there were many forests in his neighborhood.

A loud rustling over his shoulder startled him. It was Hiriam. Hiriam had a quiet conversation with Clovor, Donold, and Judah, and then took off again.

"Ok… we're headed east," Clovor said. "I'd like to get twenty miles in before nightfall."

Toby groaned. *Twenty miles?!*

Clovor pulled Deckor aside and said, loudly enough for Toby to hear, "You stay with Toby from here on out. No matter what, you always stay with Toby." Deckor nodded.

Then Deckor turned to Toby and said, "Here we go, my friend. Watch out for snakes, bats, wolves… and trolls!"

"Great!" muttered Toby.

And with that, Toby Baxter's Quest entered the forest.

CHAPTER 14

Into the Woods

The group made its way into the forest mostly in silence, which was fine with Toby. Living in a suburb, he didn't get out into the woods much. In fact, he couldn't remember ever having spent a significant amount of time hiking in a forest. The experience, in spite of the danger they were walking into, was almost otherworldly. The sounds of their feet on the fallen leaves and branches, birds singing, and animals scurrying, almost hypnotized him.

While he kept his eye out for snakes, bats, and wolves, the day so far was thankfully uneventful. The group stopped every ninety minutes or so to rest, drink, and eat. The food in their backpacks was simple but energizing, and included cheeses, breads, and dried meats. Water was the drink of the journey, instead of the elven concoction Toby had grown to like.

Surprisingly, his feet held up well. The boots were working their magic. His legs grew weary and his back was getting sore from carrying the admittedly light backpack, but overall, so far so good. At least he was keeping up.

Because the forest was so dense it was nearly impossible for Toby to have any sense of the time. He could tell it was daylight, but barely.

He was, however, able to notice that Phoenix was wearing a dark blue—or perhaps purple—football jersey with the number 10 printed on the back, and across the shoulders, the name *Tarkenton*.

"Who is Tar-ken-TON?" Toby asked.

"It's TAR-ken-ton, or Fran Tarkenton, also known as Sir Francis. He was another of the great NFL Quarterbacks. He played with the Minnesota Vikings in the 1960s and 1970s of your world. He was known as the Scrambler for his ability to run away from would-be tacklers. He led the Vikes to three Superbo..." Phoenix threw both of his hands over his mouth and suddenly looked around worriedly.

"Oh, come on Phoenix! We're headed into an epic battle with the trolls and you're worried about those football guys getting upset with you over saying the word, Superb..." Phoenix then threw his hand over Toby's mouth, looking anxiously about him once again.

After a moment or two Phoenix removed his hand from Toby's mouth and Toby began to cough.

"Are you OK, Toby?"

"*Cough, cough, cough, Super, cough, cough, cough, Bowl, cough, cough.*"

Phoenix grew wide-eyed and his body tensed, waiting for something horrible to happen to them.

"See," Toby said, "Nothing happe..." And with that Toby tripped over a log and face-planted into the ground, scraping his nose in the process. He didn't find it nearly as hilarious as Phoenix did. And to make matters worse, he scraped one of his hands on the ground and the other hand landed in something soft... and stinky! Horrifically stinky! Poop!

Toby jumped to his feet. "Hand wipe! I need a hand wipe!"

Phoenix dangled one just out of Toby's reach, still laughing hysterically.

Toby finally grabbed the hand wipe and washed off his hand until the hand wipe disintegrated, as he looked down at the pile of poop.

"That's a huge poop pile. And the smell is disgusting! What kind of animal would leave that behind?"

"Probably a dragon," suggested Phoenix.

"A dragon? Really? In the woods?"

"No! It's not dragon manure." Donold had joined them. "It's troll feces. They've been here. Recently, by the looks of it."

"Troll poop?! Gross! I need another wipe! Now!"

Clovor walked up. "OK, party's over! Stay alert!"

The long trek continued, with Toby on high alert as ordered. Every sound startled him. Every birdcall caused him to duck—*did I just step into a pun?*—until he finally relaxed, getting into somewhat of a zone, his mind keeping count with each step.

An hour or so later a rustling in the woods caught his attention. A moment after that he saw something, at least he thought he did. He heard the rustling again off to his right along with what sounded like laughing… a male laugh? He quickly turned to look and was sure he had seen a flash of something red running through the trees. He noticed Deckor looking in the same area. Deckor smiled at him and kept on walking, apparently unconcerned.

Finally, the group stopped for the day. Small canopies were set up for shelter. A fire was lit, which Toby hoped was for heat and cooking, not to keep away bats and wolves. Donold headed off into the forest and returned thirty minutes later with some dead rabbits.

Toby had never eaten rabbit before but he'd heard the old joke: It tastes like chicken. And, to his delight, it did.

It was now completely dark. The fire was the only source of light. The group sat in a circle around the fire, eating without talking, tired from a long day.

Clovor finally interrupted the quiet. "We have another big day tomorrow. And tomorrow our journey will become more challenging as we get closer to the trolls' border," she explained. "According to Hiriam we have another fifteen miles or so before we start entering the region patrolled by the trolls. Although, as we've seen, they've expanded their patrol area."

Phoenix caught Toby's attention, pinched his nose, and laughed.

"We'll have more information tomorrow," Clovor continued. "Until then, I suggest we all get some sleep. Donold and Judah, will you take the first watch?"

Toby raised his hand, then put it down again remembering he wasn't in school. "I want to do my fair share. But I'm afraid I'll fall asleep if I don't take the first watch. Might Deckor and I do the first watch? And... how long is a watch?"

Deckor groaned. He whispered to Toby, "I was hoping we'd get out of it!"

"Yes, Toby, you and Deckor may have the first watch. I know how much Deckor likes to sit quietly for three hours staring at a fire listening for strange noises," Clovor said.

"Three hours!?" Toby joined Deckor in groaning.

Before their watch began Toby asked to be excused to find a place to relieve himself. For some reason the long walk had moved things internally a bit faster than was normal for him. He grabbed his backpack, shovel, and a torch and walked a distance into the woods, with Deckor not far behind.

Toby found a log that suited him and squatted over it. Once again, he was grateful for the hand wipes. He remembered the troll poop and shivered, both from disgust and fear.

As he was shoveling over his masterpiece, he heard a noise close by. Just as he turned his head toward the sound, he found himself flat on his back with two huge green eyes attached to a big snout staring at him. The animal pinned him to the ground with both paws. Toby knew it was a wolf even though all he could see were its eyes and snout. He felt he was about to leave another masterpiece, this time in his pants, when the wolf opened its huge mouth and licked Toby from his chin to his forehead.

"Good boy!" Toby heard someone say. "Off!" and immediately the wolf moved away from Toby. Another face looked down into his, lit up by a fire torch. It was a small man, wearing a red pointy hat, his face covered in a white beard, like an Amish beard—no mustache—and wearing a red shirt and blue pants.

No way! Toby thought. *Is this a gnome? That's not what they really look like, is it? He's just like our neighbor's lawn gnome!*

He heard Deckor laughing in the background.

"Ho, Friend Gnome. My name is Deckor of the *RiverHome* Elves. We are well met. And this is one of my traveling companions, Toby Baxter, he of the Sword in the stone."

"Ho, Friend Deckor. I am Jerry. A hearty welcome to you, and to you, Master Sword Wielder. But I already know who you are, Toby Baxter!"

Toby stood up, brushed off his clothes, and wiped his face. "Actually, I don't have the Sword, or any sword for that matter. And how do you know who I am?" But without waiting for an answer he turned to Deckor and said, "And why didn't you warn me that I was about to be licked by a wolf?"

Deckor laughed. "Friend Jerry here has been tracking us for most of the afternoon. We waved at each other a few times. We know the gnomes to be our friends. And we know their wolves to be friendly, gentle, and, when need be, great warriors. I thought you might enjoy meeting them in a memorable way." Deckor and Jerry high-fived each other. Jerry had to stand on his tiptoes to do so as he was slightly shorter than Deckor.

"Very funny!" Toby deadpanned.

"Come, Friend Jerry," Deckor said. "We have much to discuss."

"Yes, we do, Friend Deckor. I'm afraid evil is closer than you realize." Jerry then yelled, "Heel, Saaba!" and with that Saaba the Wolf fell in line behind Jerry, Deckor, and Toby.

When they got back to camp, they found the rest of the group sitting around the fire laughing. In the middle of the group sat another gnome, but this one didn't have a beard. Instead, she had long, blonde hair with a bright blue pointy hat sitting on top of her head. She was clothed in a blue tunic and red pants... or slacks... or whatever girls wear. She was obviously the center of attention and the reason for the laughter. Sitting next to her was a huge wolf, about the same size as Saaba.

All eyes turned to Toby, Deckor, Jerry, and Saaba the Wolf.

"Well met, Friend Gnome!" Judah shouted as he motioned for them to join the group at the fire.

Once they were seated on various logs and stones—*not nearly as comfy as movie theater recliners*—introductions were made.

"This is Friend Jerry of the Gnomes," Deckor said. "And this is his wolf, Saaba."

"This is my daughter, Roxie," Jerry said, "and this is her wolf, Saanti."

"We are honored to be visited by our friends the Gnomes," Clovor said. It all seemed rather formal to Toby but no one else appeared bothered by it.

"I hate to dampen your levity. I know my daughter to be quite the story-teller!"

"Indeed she is!" gushed Phoenix. Phoenix flashed a quick glance at Roxie and she responded with a sheepish smile. Did Toby detect a spark of interest between the two of them? Saanti's growl hinted that the wolf wasn't all that keen about it. *Keen? Where are these words coming from?*

"Tell us what you've seen and heard, Friend Jerry," Donold said.

"There has been a lot of troll activity this far west of their stronghold. That's unusual. We were able to capture one of their spies. After an intense interrogation we pried some information out of him."

Toby gasped. *Interrogations? What did that mean? Thumbscrews? Sleep deprivation? Nails on a chalkboard? Force feeding Brussel—or is it Brussels—sprouts?* Whatever it was, he did not sign up for this.

Roxie saw the concern on Toby's face and smiled. Her smile lit up her face. He could understand why Phoenix sat over there with that gaga look on his face.

"Don't worry, Friend Toby. We don't torture or harm anyone. It's not in our nature. We have developed a very potent, but delicious and good-for-you shake, that essentially opens you up to truth telling."

"It comes in three fantastic flavors, by the way," Jerry chimed in. "Vanilla, Dark Chocolate—my favorite—and Strawberry/Banana. You should try it."

"I'll take your word for it," said Toby. He wasn't sure if he was hiding any secrets but he wasn't in the mood to chance it.

"Please continue," urged Donold, obviously anxious to know where the group stood in terms of the trolls.

"The now truth-telling troll spy filled us in on Clygon's plan." He looked at Toby as he said it and Toby felt a chill run up and down his spine, causing him to shiver. Mathilda, sitting next to him, reached out her hand and placed it on his.

"I'm sorry, Friend Toby, but Clygon's plan is to break you."

CHAPTER 15

A Simile, a Metaphor, and a Symbol

All eyes were on Toby. "Break me?" he squeaked.

"It has to do with you and the Sword, Friend Toby. Clygon believes that if he can break you, he can break the power of the Sword."

Jerry's warning was met with an intake of breath from Mathilda.

"It all makes sense now," Clovor muttered, seemingly to herself, but loud enough for the rest to hear. "Clygon has been trying to get us to believe that we are on a Quest to defeat him. But all along this has been his Quest to…"

She let the rest of the sentence hang in the air.

So Toby finished it. "To get to me. But why? Why is he so afraid of me? Why is he so afraid of the Sword?"

"Tell him!" Judah said. "He needs to know. Tell him!"

Mathilda tightened her grip on Toby's hand. Donold stood up and walked over behind him and placed a hand on his shoulder.

This can't be good, Toby thought.

"Toby, the Sword has always stopped Clygon from totally defeating us," Clovor began. "To be sure, Clygon has won some battles…" Clovor's voice caught as she thought of her parents.

She cleared her throat and continued. "But when all seems lost, the Sword calls a Hero to fight alongside of us. So Clygon knows that he can't win as long as the Sword exists. That's why he fears the Sword. He hates the Sword. And he is determined to destroy it. Stealing the Sword is the closest he's gotten but he cannot break the power of the Sword."

"Why not?" Toby asked.

"Because it's the Hero who gives the Sword its power. And he's finally figured that out."

"I don't understand," Toby said.

Judah stepped in. "A sword is really an extension of the user. That's why the owner of a sword will often name it or will inherit a sword already named. Think about the great Quest stories. In *The Lord of the Rings,* for example, Frodo is given the Sword *Sting.* Aragorn wielded *Narsil.* Gandalph had *Glamdring.*"

"Percy Jackson had *Riptide,*" Mathilda added. "And of course, King Arthur had *Excalibur.*"

"But the Sword is magic, right? I felt its power."

"It's complicated, and a story for another time, but yes, the Sword has its own magic, of which, thankfully, Clygon is unaware," Clovor answered. "But what you need to understand in this moment, Toby, is that when it comes to battling Clygon and the trolls, you are the magic behind the Sword."

Toby stared at them blankly.

"Try this. Think of the Sword as a metaphor," Judah said. "Do you know what a metaphor is?"

"Yes. It's when something is like something else."

"Good try," Judah said, "but that's a simile."

"I'm not following."

"A simile compares one thing to another. As you said, something is like something else."

"For example," Phoenix interjected, his gaga face locked in on Roxie. "She is like an angel." Roxie blushed. Saanti growled. Phoenix was oblivious.

"Yes, thank you, Phoenix," Judah deadpanned. "A metaphor," he continued, "says that one thing is not just like another thing but *is* another thing."

"Huh?"

Again, Phoenix chimed in: "She is an angel." Another Roxie blush. Another Saanti growl, this time baring a few teeth. And a still oblivious Phoenix.

"It's raining cats and dogs. That's a metaphor. It's a picture of a downpour," Judah reinserted himself once again. "Obviously it doesn't literally rain cats and dogs."

"Sorry. It still makes no sense to me."

"How about this," Jerry said. "The Sword is a symbol of your power. It's not your actual power. It represents your power."

"What power?"

"Your growing power as a man, of course, Friend Toby."

"How many times do I have to tell you? I'm only thirteen! I'm just a kid."

"But, Friend Toby, in many cultures in your world, that's the time when a boy is considered a man."

"Well, I don't know about other cultures in my world, but in my country, if boys grow into men at all, it's well into their twenties and thirties. At least that's what some of the girls in my class told me."

Jerry laughed. "That's a good one, Friend Toby. But seriously…"

"I was being serious," Toby said.

But Jerry continued on as if he hadn't heard him. "... thirteen has always marked a significant moment in the life of a boy, that moment when he begins to turn from boyhood to manhood. That moment when he begins to discover and develop his growing power as a man."

"What is this power you keep talking about?"

"It's different for every man. A man's power is his passion. His compassion. His gifts. His skills. His talents. His morals and values. His faith. It's all of those things, used together, that make a man powerful. And the Sword is the symbol of that. Through that Sword all of your powers come to life. Perhaps," Jerry looked at Clovor, "that's a part of its magic."

Toby's head was spinning. He'd just celebrated his thirteenth birthday—*when was that?*—and now he was supposed to act like a man?

"How does breaking me break the Sword?" he asked.

Clovor answered. "The question every Hero must face when wielding the Sword is this: *How will you use your power?*"

Toby gasped.

"What is it?" Deckor asked.

"When I first put my hands on the Sword during that rain storm, I heard a voice ask the same question. And it sounded like the voice of my grandfather: *How will you use your power?* I heard it again the other night."

Clovor nodded. "Toby, only you can answer that question. But remember this: Your power, your Sword, was given to you to make the world a better place. To serve others. To protect the ones you love. Clygon will use every trick he can to get you to misuse your power. To use it violently. To use it selfishly. To use it to destroy. And, *if* you do that, he will break you. And that, in turn, will break the Sword and its power to hold Clygon back."

Clovor held Toby's eyes with hers. "Toby, we will not abandon you. We will fight with you and fight for you. We will mentor you the best that we can. But when the moment comes, only you can choose how you will use your power. Use it wisely."

As Toby listened to her something popped, metaphorically speaking, in his brain.

"Who were the other Heroes?" he asked her.

"I think you have already figured it out."

"Tell me."

"Before you, the Hero called to help us in the Troll War was Thomas Baxter, your father. And before him, Titus Baxter, your grandfather. And before him, Tyler Baxter, your great-grandfather. All of them were called here by the Sword. Each of them faced the challenge of how he would use his Sword… his power. But this time is different, Toby. This time Clygon has changed his tactics from fighting a war against us to fighting the Hero… to fighting you."

Toby stared into the fire. Mathilda let go of his hand. Donold removed his hand from Toby's shoulder and sat down.

"So… all we need to do," Toby said, "is somehow sneak into the troll camp, grab the Sword, wherever it is, discover my super powers, and then figure out how to not let Clygon break me. Fantastic!"

"Yup… that's about it," Deckor said as he patted Toby on the back.

"Toby Baxter. Look at me!" Clovor commanded.

As Toby looked into her eyes once again she said, "Like your father and grandfather and great-grandfather before you, you will meet this challenge, Toby Baxter. You have been called by the Sword. You have been marked by the elves. You have been created for this moment. I believe in you. We believe in you."

With that, everyone stood up. One by one, elf and gnome, walked by Toby and either shook his hand or hugged him. Even Saaba and Saanti walked over to him, jumped up, putting their paws on his shoulders, and licked his face.

"Toby, Donold and I will take the first watch. You've had enough for one day. Try to get some sleep. The Healer will bring you some of our sleep draught if you want it," Judah said.

Toby wanted it. And he told the Healer so.

But even with the sleep draught, Toby had a hard time falling asleep. He wondered how he would use his power, whatever that power was, when it mattered. And with that thought he finally fell into a fitful sleep.

CHAPTER 16

On the Run

It was the hand on his mouth that woke him. Or maybe it was the low growl of Saaba the Wolf, who apparently had come to sleep next to him. Deckor's face was two inches from Toby's face. Had Deckor not been holding a small torch, Toby would have had no idea who was standing over him, as it was still dark outside.

"Don't make a sound, Toby. We need to go. Now! Trolls!" Deckor whispered.

That was all Toby needed to hear. He grabbed his backpack and quietly followed Deckor out of the tent, with Saaba right behind them. Toby could see his friends running around, swords raised, bows and arrows at the ready, with several gnomes... *where did they come from?*... holding torches so that they could see what they were fighting. Clovor ran over, a fierce look on her face. Fear? Determination?

Looking at Toby, she said to Deckor, "Get him out of here. Jerry and Roxie will guide you. They know where to go. Find that Sword and get it into Toby's hands. We'll join you as soon as we can."

Deckor looked like he was about to argue, but Clovor shot him a glance so severe that Deckor simply nodded in agreement. And just like that Clovor was off. It appeared to Toby that the elves and gnomes were forming a circle with their backs to each other. A defensive move, perhaps? He shook his head. How would he know?

He felt tugging on his sleeve. He looked down and saw Roxie. She was sitting on Saanti's back. "Climb on Toby, and hang on."

Before he could argue she grabbed him by the arm and pulled him onto the back of the wolf. Roxie's strength caught him by surprise.

"What do I hang on to?" he said.

"My waist. And do it now!" she yelled.

Toby quickly threw his arms around her tiny waist and bent his legs at the knees as Roxie gave a short whistle. Saanti took off through the woods, followed by Saaba, carrying Jerry and Deckor.

Toby risked a look over his shoulder to check on his friends. And that's when he caught his first glimpse of a troll, eerily lit by a nearby torch. It was about his height. But from his quick glance it looked to be as wide as it was tall. It had hair growing out of its ears and elbows. Its skin looked like that of an elephant or rhino. It had overly-large ears and a huge, crooked nose. And biceps to spare! In its right hand was a sword. In its left hand it held a club. And it was headed straight toward Mathilda.

At that moment Saanti swerved left and Toby almost fell off of the wolf. But Roxie grabbed his arm and helped him settle back down on Saanti's back. He could no longer see his friends.

And then, to make matters worse, he heard the terrifying, shrieking battle cry of the trolls.

I WARNED YOU TOBY BAXTER. NOW YOUR FATE HAS BEEN SEALED. I'M WAITING FOR YOU!

The shriek turned into a blood-curdling laugh.

Toby tightened his grip on Roxie, and as he did so the fingers on his left hand could feel the elven marking Grandpa had placed on his right hand. It provided some comfort that he would see his friends again. That somehow they would survive that attack by the trolls.

Saaba and Saanti continued to run full speed through the forest. It was still dark and Toby wondered how they didn't run into trees and kill them all. From time to time even Roxie tensed as they leapt over one log, only to make a sharp turn to the right followed by a sharp swerve to the left. On a rollercoaster this might be fun. But when running for one's life, not so much.

"Keep your head down," Roxie yelled to Toby. "We wouldn't want to leave it behind on a low hanging branch."

"Very funny," he yelled back into her ear. He wanted to ask how it was that her hat stayed on her head, but another quick swerve by Saanti forced him to swallow the question.

The wolves ran for what seemed like hours. Toby marveled at their incredible stamina. He could see daylight seeping through the trees, and suddenly the loss of sleep and the comedown from the adrenaline rush overwhelmed him. He was exhausted. He could barely keep his eyes open.

Just when he was about to nod off the pace of the wolves slowed. Then it fell to a walk. And then they halted. Before them Toby saw a huge clearing in the woods with small huts built in a circle facing each other. In the middle of the circle was a large fire pit with benches around it.

The small village was alive with activity. Gnomes running back and forth, busily doing whatever they were doing until one of them spotted the two wolves and their passengers. Then all the gnomes stopped to look at them.

"Is that Toby Baxter?" he heard someone ask.

How would they know who I am? he wondered.

Toby watched as Jerry and Roxie jumped off of the wolves and quickly ran around to face them. Jerry put his forehead onto Saaba's forehead and Roxie did the same with Saanti. The wolves were heaving with exhaustion, but seemed to calm the longer Jerry and Roxie held their foreheads to those of their wolves.

Toby found that he couldn't move. His legs were dead. His body numb. Six gnomes ran over to him and gently lifted him off of Saanti and carried him toward the huts. A female gnome met them at the door and pointed to a bed. They laid Toby on it—the softest bed he'd ever experienced, even though his legs dangled over it from his knees on down. The woman put a blanket over him and headed for the door. She was about to close it from the outside when Saaba walked in and curled up next to him. And within moments Toby and Saaba the Wolf were fast asleep.

He had no idea how long he had slept but when he woke up it was bright and sunny outside. Saaba was still asleep next to him. Toby got up as quietly as he could so as not to wake the wolf. Not quietly enough. Saaba opened one eye, looked at him, and then fell back to sleep.

Toby walked out of the hut, having to shield his eyes from the bright sun. Gnomes were scurrying all around the village doing who knows what. Little gnomes, or better said, littler gnomes—he assumed they were children—were playing Frisbee of all things! A Frisbee came flying right at him, landing at his feet. The children stopped, unsure what to do. Toby reached down, picked up the Frisbee, and sent it flying back to the kids. He was good at Frisbee, come to think of it. But that didn't seem to be the kind of superhero power he would need to take on trolls.

He noticed Deckor, Roxie, Jerry, and an elderly gnome huddled together on one of the benches by the fire pit. Deckor saw him and waved him over.

"Hiriam was here. You just missed him. He didn't have much to report as that traitor Demetrius is patrolling the skies. He did say that we can't stay here long as the trolls are close. The gnomes are getting ready to move."

That explained the scurrying.

"Did he say anything about Clovor and the others?"

Deckor shook his head no. Toby could tell he was as concerned as Toby himself was.

They sat quietly for a moment when Jerry sat up. "Please forgive my lack of hospitality, Friend Toby. This is our Chieftain, Ernest. Ernest, this is Toby Baxter."

"You are well met, Friend Toby, although I wish the times were better met."

"Thank you." That was all Toby could think of to say.

"We've decided that the two of us need to leave tonight, as soon as darkness hits," Deckor said. "We are about thirty-five miles from where we believe Clygon's camp is. And for the safety of the gnomes we need to distance ourselves from them."

Toby nodded.

"But we will not abandon you, Toby," Jerry said. "Apparently Wolf Saaba has become quite fond of you, and even protective. He will stay with you, Friend Toby."

Now Toby really had no idea what to do or say. The tears in his eyes said enough for the rest of them. Roxie reached up and grabbed him around the chest and gave him a hug.

"You bear a great burden, Friend Toby. But you do not bear it alone!"

Again they sat quietly for a few moments. Toby realized there had been many of these quiet, silent moments since he'd arrived in this world. He listened to the laughing of the children, oblivious to the danger around them. He listened to the sounds of the birds chirping in the warm sunshine. And then a thought hit him, metaphorically speaking.

"I want to see the troll. He's here, right? The one you captured?"

They all stared at him.

"I want to see the troll," he said again. "I need to look him in the eyes. I need to face the fear. I need to know who it is who wants to break me… to break us. I want to see the troll."

Chieftain Ernest nodded. "Yes, Friend Toby. You of all people deserve to see him. Follow me."

CHAPTER 17

Face to Face with a Troll

Chieftain Ernest led Toby, Deckor, Jerry and Roxie, followed by Saanti, to one of the huts. Two gnomes stood guard by the door with swords drawn. When Toby was ushered into the room he took in several things at once.

The troll was sitting at a table with what seemed like a banquet in front of him. He was so busy stuffing his face that he didn't notice his guests.

Like the troll he'd quickly glimpsed yesterday—*or was that earlier this morning?*—this troll, too, appeared to be the same height as Toby, although the troll was sitting so it was hard to tell. Like the other troll, this troll was sturdily built with big muscles. His skin was grayish and rough-looking, with tufts of hair sticking out of it. Its head was covered in what looked like brown straw sticking up every which way. It had an overly-large nose and big ears. It wore what appeared to be an animal fur robe loosely hanging over its body.

Toby also noticed the smell. Mixed in with the pleasing aromas of the troll's banquet was the smell of sweat and vomit. Toby had to fight back a gag.

He felt immediate hatred for this troll. Not the kind of hatred he had for Seattle Seahawks Fans. That was a hatred built on envy. The Seahawks usually ended up better in the standings than his team. *But not always!* he reminded himself. Plus, he didn't really hate Seahawks fans in the sense of hatred. It was more a form of begrudging respect.

But this was different. It was the first time in his life when Toby felt a deep-seated sense of outrage, anger, and disgust toward someone or something. Even worse than his utter dislike of Derrick. Everything in him wanted to run at the troll and beat it to a pulp.

Jerry cleared his throat to get the troll's attention. It looked up—Toby could only think of it as an "it" rather than as a "he" or a person—taking in its guests. But when it saw Toby, it leapt from its chair and backed up hard into the wall, terror on its face. Toby felt a thrill of joy in that moment.

"Wha… wh… what do you want, Toby Baxter?" it stammered.

But Toby remained silent. He was enjoying seeing this weasel squirm. He never knew hatred could feel this good. This powerful.

The troll made for his chair but Toby took a step toward it, causing it to let out a gasp and move back against the wall again. Toby thought that he could get used to this. If this is all it was going to take to defeat the trolls, he was all in.

"Toby… Toby…" he could hear Deckor whispering in his ear. "Toby… are you OK?"

Still Toby said nothing. He could tell that made the troll squirm all the more.

He turned to leave the room. He'd seen the enemy and the mystery was gone. So was the fear.

Before Toby got to the door the troll cried out: "Your father was weak!"

Toby had no idea how it happened, but the next thing he knew he was holding the troll by its throat across the table, a dagger in his other hand pointed at the big vein in the disgusting creature's neck. A small amount of blood seeped out of a tiny wound Toby had apparently put there.

"Toby! Stop!" Roxie screamed.

How will you use your power? His grandpa's voice rang in his ears.

And then the troll did something that shook Toby to his core. It relaxed. Then it smiled. An evil, wicked smile.

"Very good, Toby Baxter. Very good!" it said, quiet enough so that only Toby could hear. "Now we have you exactly where we want you. Clygon will be thrilled to see you."

Toby let go of the troll and dropped his dagger onto the floor. His head was spinning.

He pushed his way out of the hut, the troll's laughter following him outside.

Toby leaned up against the wall of the hut and then slid down, landing on his butt.

Chieftain Ernest, Jerry, Roxie, and Deckor stood around him with Saanti off to the side.

"Are you OK, Friend Toby?" Jerry asked.

"Why are you feeding that monster a banquet? Why isn't he locked up in chains? You're treating him like a guest of honor!" Toby spit out the words in anger.

Chieftain Ernest answered. "Toby, it is our code as gnomes to practice kindness to our enemies, to try to win them over. Violence is always our last resort. We were hoping that he might turn and help us. But I'm afraid that may not happen now."

"Toby…" Roxie said.

"Go away! Now! Leave me alone!"

The four of them, along with Saanti, left Toby to himself. And to himself Toby was appalled at what he had just done. *Where did that hatred come from?* he wondered. *Is that really the kind of person I am? Is that how I'm going to use my power?* He was disgusted with himself. But that wasn't really true. He was afraid of himself.

He'd been sitting alone for about fifteen minutes when Deckor came over and sat down beside him. Deckor handed him the dagger Toby had dropped on the floor.

After several quiet moments Toby asked, "Did you know my father?"

"Yes, I did."

"Was he weak like that troll said?"

"No, Toby. Your dad proved to be a good, valiant young man. The troll was trying to get under your skin, and seemed to do a pretty good job of it. Do you want to talk about it?"

Toby didn't want to talk about it so he kept to the topic of his dad. "Why didn't my dad ever tell me about his time here? I get the sense he doesn't even remember it."

"Sometimes the memories of our world fade over time in your world. But what happens to you here will continue to influence you for the rest of your life. The decisions you make and the experiences you have here will play an important role in shaping the man you will become. Most of those decisions you will forget, but they will stay with you in the kind of person and man you are."

"You mean, someday I will forget all of this? I will forget all of you?"

"I can't say for sure, Toby. But I can say that we will never forget you."

Toby stared down at the ground. The energy of the anger and hatred, and of what he had done to the troll with the dagger, still churned within him.

"Your great-grandpa was called here when he turned fourteen."

"Fourteen?"

"Each boy begins the Quest into manhood differently. Your grandpa had just turned twelve. Your dad, thirteen. You, of course, thirteen as well. But it's usually within a few years of thirteen. The Sword called your dad at the beginning of the Troll War. Like you, he was scared, confused, and a bit lost. That's the way of it. That's why you need guides and friends, Toby. You can't make this journey alone."

"So… what happened to my dad?"

"That's his story to tell, Toby."

"But I told you, he doesn't seem to remember it."

"I have a hunch he will soon!"

And with that mysterious prediction Toby looked up and noticed that all of the gnome huts had been dismantled with the exception of two—the one holding the troll and the one Toby had slept in.

"How did they do that so fast?" Toby asked.

"Gnome ingenuity! They've learned how to be fast packers. They will head off in an hour or so. In the meantime, you need to get some sleep. We need to go soon, too. The trolls aren't far away."

"What will happen to that monster in there?" Toby nodded toward the hut holding the troll.

"The gnomes will take him with them in the hope of maybe getting more information out of him."

"I really blew it, didn't I? I have no idea what came over me," Toby said.

"How about you get a few hours of sleep. We'll have plenty of time to talk about it tonight. And we need to talk about it before we get to the trolls' stronghold."

Deckor led Toby back to his hut. Jerry, Saaba, Roxie, and Saanti were waiting for him.

"Friend Toby, we must take our leave now," Jerry said. "May the Creator guide you and keep you safe."

He stuck out his hand and shook Toby's hand and did the same with Deckor. Roxie jumped up and hugged him. "Goodbye… for now… Friend Toby. I believe in you!"

Toby watched as Jerry bent down to Saaba, holding the wolf's head in his hands. Toby could see Jerry's shoulders bobbing up and down. He was weeping. And it seemed as if Saaba was, too.

"Keep him safe, Friend Toby, and bring him back to me," Jerry said.

"He really is staying with me?" Toby asked, incredulous.

"Yes, Friend Toby," Jerry said through his tears.

And with that Jerry, Roxie, and Saanti walked away and Toby, Deckor, and Saaba headed into the hut to catch a couple of hours of sleep.

CHAPTER 18

A Costly Miscalculation

But Deckor got it wrong. They didn't have a few hours.

Saaba heard it first and growled. Then Deckor heard it and grabbed his sword. And finally, Toby heard it.

Trolls!

A fist pounded on the door. "We know you are in there, Toby Baxter! Come on out. Clygon invites you to his palace for a banquet in your honor." They heard laughter. Lots of laughter. Lots of trolls.

Deckor pointed his head in the direction of the back of the hut. Toby saw a small door. He quietly moved toward it and was about to open it when Saaba moved past him. The wolf then nodded at Toby, as if giving the OK to open the door. Toby did so, only to be met with a volcanic explosion of sweat and vomit. The trolls were waiting for them.

Saaba growled at them and was about to pounce through the door, but Toby stopped him. "Heel, Saaba. It's no use. They outnumber us." And then he leaned down and whispered into Saaba's ear. "When they come in to grab us, run and find Clovor!"

One big, hairy, mean-looking troll walked in through the front door and another one, even meaner looking, squeezed through the back door.

Immediately Saaba flew out the door, much to the surprise of the trolls out back. But they weren't fast enough and Saaba was gone into the woods.

Deckor laid down his sword and put up his hands. Toby did the same with his dagger and his hands. He watched in horror as the front door troll sledge-hammered Deckor on the head, knocking him out cold.

And then the darkness engulfed Toby Baxter.

He had no idea what time it was when he came to, but it was dark. He had a splitting headache. And to make matters worse, he was sitting with his back against a tree. A chain wrapped around the tree was attached to each of his wrists, stretching both of his arms behind him. Pain shot down his shoulders and arms, and into his hands.

He heard Deckor moaning next to him. Deckor, too, was chained to a tree in the same way. Toby saw that Deckor's right eye was swollen to the point of being closed and that his lip was cut, with dry blood on his chin.

Then he heard another sound, and his heart sank. Looking to his left he saw Saaba, chained to a stake in the ground, and muzzled. It was obvious that the wolf had been in a fight. Blood-streaked gashes lined his body. Saaba whined a bit as he looked at Toby.

More noises entered his consciousness. Laughing. Talking. Arguing. More laughing. He looked past Saaba and saw about twenty trolls standing around fires. They seemed to be eating and Toby realized that, in spite of his pain, he was hungry.

Toby turned his attention back to Deckor. "Are you OK?" he asked. "What happened to your face?"

Deckor laughed and said, "You should see what my face did to that troll's hand!" He coughed several times and Toby could tell that Deckor's ribs had taken a shot as well.

"Do you know where we are?"

"Obviously in a troll camp, but where… I have no idea. I haven't been able to make out what they're saying."

Saaba's whimper alerted them. A troll was approaching. Toby didn't need the warning. He could smell the sweat and vomit coming toward him. He wanted to gag but he was too tired.

"Well, well, well! A River Elf, a gnome's wolf, and a Hero. What do you know! Sounds like the beginning of a good joke. Hey, Plythar, come on over and have a look at *The* Toby Baxter."

A squat, fat troll waddled over. He looked Toby over a few times then gave a hard kick to Toby's foot.

Toby looked up at him and felt the hate taking over again. And as it did, Plythar smiled. "This will please Clygon!"

"What do you want?" Toby demanded.

"Pretty tough there in your chains, aren't you little boy," the first troll taunted. "I just sauntered over to ask if you, your elven friend here, and your wolf, might be hungry. We may be trolls. We may be your enemies. But we do know how to treat our guests well."

Toby stared at him defiantly.

"Sir. Thank you. We would appreciate whatever food you might offer us," Deckor said.

Toby shot him the evil-eye but Deckor continued. "If it wouldn't be too much of a bother."

The troll laughed. "Now those are good manners. Thank you, River Elf, for being so polite. We will have your feast brought to you in a few moments." The troll thought that was funny and walked away laughing, along with Plythar.

"What was that about?" Toby asked Deckor.

"Survival, Toby. And if I may, you might want to get a handle on that anger. A warrior is no good when he's ruled by rage."

Toby opened his mouth to speak, and then shut it. That rage and anger made him feel powerful and ugly at the same time. *But in the face of an enemy doesn't one need to harness anger and rage to fight?* he wondered.

Moments later the troll and Plythar returned. "Here you go." They threw down three bowls, one each in front of Toby, Deckor, and Saaba.

"What is it?" Toby asked as politely as he could.

"Rabbit stew. Without the rabbit," the troll said, laughing.

"Sir," Deckor said, "we are very grateful. But I'm not sure how we're supposed to eat this feast with our hands chained behind us."

"No worries, River Elf." The troll clapped his hands and three trolls left one of the fires and ran over to them. "These three will feed you!"

"Thank you, sir," Deckor said. "But is there anyway we might have the chains loosened, at least for a few moments. Our arms and shoulders have gone numb. And Toby Baxter here will be no good to you, or to Clygon, if his sword arm is permanently damaged."

"Good point, River Elf. After you eat, I'll see what I can do. Bon appetite!"

Bon appetite? Toby muttered quietly. *Isn't it supposed to be bon appetit? And when did I suddenly become a French Chef?*

As the troll and Plythar walked back to the fires, the three trolls began to feed the broth to Toby, Deckor, and Saaba. Their troll breath smelled of vomit and the broth tasted like urine, although Toby had no experience with tasting urine. He gagged down each spoonful, knowing he needed at least some nourishment. He could tell that Saaba was having a tough time eating the broth through the muzzle.

Moments later, after the trolls had finished feeding them, Toby felt something churning in his gut. Without warning he threw up all of the broth, and then some bile, and then probably a part of his stomach. It splattered all over his legs. And it reeked!

His head ached. His arms were numb. He smelled of puke. His friends were chained up. He was angry. He wanted to scream.

Then two things happened at once. His arms fell to the ground, released from the chains, and a huge bucket of ice-cold water was thrown at him. The water took his breath away.

"Hey, what was that about?" he sputtered to the troll who had doused him. But the troll turned and walked away without saying a word.

He looked over and saw that Deckor had been unchained as well. He thought that perhaps Deckor had lost consciousness as he sat limp against the tree. But soon Deckor started to move his arms, evidently trying to get the blood flowing through them again.

Saaba was still chained to the stake, the muzzle still on his snout. But he was sitting up.

The first troll, the one who seemed to be in charge of the others, approached them. "Ah, I see Sir Toby Baxter has had a bath. Good. Needed to wash off your dinner!" The troll laughed. Toby didn't.

"Lighten up, Hero! We're going to be spending the next day or two together." He reached out his hand to Toby to lift him to his feet but Toby preferred to stand up by himself. The problem was, he couldn't. So he begrudgingly took the troll's hand. It felt like course sandpaper. As the troll roughly lifted Toby to his feet he said, "My name, by the way, is Blythar. And yup, you guessed it. Plythar is my brother."

Blythar helped Deckor to his feet and then unhooked Saaba from the stake, making sure he had a good hold of the chain so that the wolf couldn't escape.

"Follow me!" he said gruffly.

Blythar led them to one of the fires. "Sit here. Stand here. Stand on your head here. I don't care. But stick close to the fire so we can see you. And dry off. We don't want the Hero here getting sick on us."

But Toby thought Blythar might be too late. He was chilled. He felt feverish. He wanted to wake up and go home.

Deckor and Toby sat on one of the wood logs and moved as close to the fire as they could. Saaba was next to them, staked to the ground. Toby removed Saaba's muzzle and Saaba returned the favor by curling up at Toby's feet.

They sat quietly for a long time, lost in their thoughts. The fire was warm. It made Toby sleepy.

He finally broke the silence. "Deckor?"

"No, I don't!"

"Don't what?"

"Have a plan!"

"That's not what I was going to ask."

"Sorry. I'm not much of a protector, am I?"

Toby let the comment pass. "How old are you? At times you seem like a young man. At other times you seem old enough to be my dad."

Deckor chuckled, if that was what you would call his rib-protecting laugh. "Our time, as you know, works differently than your time does. A moment in your world may last an hour, a day, a week, or even months in our world. Quite honestly, there doesn't seem to be any rhyme or reason to it. We grow to be quite old in our years. In terms of your world, I could very well be as old as your dad. Perhaps a bit older. But in my world, I am, as you sensed, a young man, perhaps nineteen or twenty of your years old? I've seen a lot of life in those years."

Toby assumed Deckor was thinking about the death of his parents.

"Have you ever seen a dragon?"

"What?"

"When Judah was telling the story about the creation of your world, he mentioned dragons. Have you ever seen one?"

"Once. Dragons don't tend to venture into our part of the world. But I did see one once. I was on a long hunting expedition with a group of River Elves. One day I saw a huge shadow cross over our path. I looked up and there it was. A beautiful, huge, green dragon. It was majestic. It spotted us and swooped around our little group three times as if checking us out… or showing off. The closer it got the more magnificent it was. The scales on its body looked more like feathers. It's big yellow eyes actually looked friendly… or curious… or amused. It seemed like it wanted to talk to us, which is ridiculous, of course, because dragons don't talk. It flew so close we could almost touch it and then it rocketed back up into the sky and vanished."

Deckor paused, reliving the experience. "It was a sacred moment, Toby."

Toby understood. He'd had the same experience on a family trip to Hawaii when he'd seen a whale breach. He hated to break the mood but he had another question. "How about unicorns? Have you ever seen one of them?"

Deckor looked at him and smiled. A big, happy smile.

"When we were kids a travelling circus of ogres came to *RiverHome*."

"A traveling ogres' circus?"

"They used to come every year. The ogres would set up a big tent and do shows. One of the ogres could bend metal. Some of the ogres did acrobatics."

Toby had never seen an ogre but he had a hard time imagining ogres on a flying trapeze.

"They even had clown ogres." Deckor shivered for a moment. "Outside of the tent they set up arcade games like Arrow Shooting or the Ring Toss. But one of the best parts of the circus was the kiddie rides. Most of them were pretty lame… like the train ride or the small Ferris wheel, but fun nonetheless.

"But one year, the biggest wonder of them all was the Unicorn ride. They had two unicorns. One male and one female. And you could ride them. You should have seen the line of kids waiting for a ride. I was one of them. They were magnificent animals. White. Long manes and tails. Beautiful silver horns. But when I got onto the male unicorn I could tell something wasn't right. I could feel sadness. I could feel despair. I felt the joy draining out of me the longer I rode the unicorn.

"When the ride was done I petted the animal on its nose. I don't know how I knew, but when I looked into its eyes I felt as if it was telling me to save him. I may have imagined it, Toby, but I saw tears in his eyes. And I had tears streaming down my cheeks. My parents thought it was because I was so moved by the chance to see and ride a unicorn.

"That night I shared my feelings with Clovor and Phoenix. They had had the exact same experience. Phoenix had ridden the male unicorn and Clovor the female. We immediately knew what to do.

"After everyone was in bed we snuck down to the circus and found the unicorns. Again, I may have imagined it, but they seemed happy to see us. We quickly opened the gate to the enclosure they were in and led them outside. We walked them down the stream path to the *River Glaedaan*. The unicorns bowed to us. Can you imagine? They bowed to us! And then they took off down the river.

"The next morning all you-know-what broke loose. The ogres demanded a search of every *RiverHome* home. But the leadership, my parents included, refused. The ogres packed up and we never saw them again.

"At dinner that night our parents nonchalantly mentioned the unicorns. They said that if anyone knew what had happened to the unicorns, the leadership of *RiverHome* unofficially thanked whomever had set them free. And mom and dad looked each one of us in the eyes and smiled.

"About a year later the unicorns appeared at the oval game field. We ran out to them and they allowed us to hug them. And behind them was a small unicorn. A son! We named the dad Hermey after…"

"Santa's Elf? The one who wanted to be a dentist? From that old stop animation Rudolph the Red Nosed Reindeer show?"

Deckor laughed. "No, although who knows, he may be a distant relative of ours. We named him Hermey after one of our great warriors from of old. We named the mom Philly after a great-great grandmother. And we named their son Rayfa after our great-grandfather. The rest of the village saw the unicorns and ran out to greet them. And then we all waved goodbye as they headed back into the forest. And that was the last time we saw them."

Deckor was once again lost in his thoughts.

"Thank you, Toby!"

"For what?"

"For asking. You gave me the gift of good memories in this place of despair."

"I don't know if this is a long, weird dream or the real thing," Toby said, "but I would love to see a dragon and a unicorn someday."

They were interrupted by Blythar and Plythar. "OK, you three. Time for bed. We have a long walk tomorrow. Destiny awaits, Hero Toby Baxter!" Blythar laughed. Toby hated that laugh.

They were led to a small tent. Two thin mattresses lay on the floor. Toby and Deckor were pushed onto them and Saaba was staked beside Toby.

"May Clygon haunt your dreams!" Plythar laughed. Toby hated his laugh, too.

The fire had done its magic and Toby felt a bit better. His head still ached. His arms were stiff but he could feel them again. And the water had at least removed the vomit from his clothes, which were now mostly dry. Before he knew it, he was asleep.

CHAPTER 19

Off to See Clygon

"Wake up, sleepy heads! Your beauty rest is over. It's time to move!" Blythar was in a bad mood.

Toby and Deckor slowly sat up. Both of them had raging headaches and their bodies were stiff and sore. Toby's stomach growled. He was hungry, but he wasn't sure he could handle another bowl of rabbit stew.

The three trolls who had "waited" on them the night before stood outside, each with a plate of food: one for Toby, one for Deckor, and one for Saaba. Each of the plates held what looked like a piece of roasted rabbit and a hunk of bread. Toby's mouth watered. He sat down, as did Deckor, and ate it all. It actually tasted good and settled his stomach. Then they were handed a cup filled with fresh water. Toby gulped down three cups' full before Plythar walked over. "That's enough. We don't have time for potty breaks today!" He, too, seemed surly. *Surly? Where did that word come from?*

It was as Toby was feeding Saaba that he caught a whiff of it. Surrounded by the noxious troll odors it stood out. Hope! Deckor smelled it, too. Both of them quickly looked at each other and then over at the trolls.

The entire troll camp stopped. They smelled it as well. But apparently it was not a pleasing aroma for them as they all began to cough and choke.

Deckor, feeling a renewed sense of courage and energy, joked to Toby, "Apparently hope smells vile to not-so-nice people."

Toby poked Deckor in the ribs and pointed his head toward the three trolls who were feeding them. Rather than choking on the smell of hope, it seemed to relax them.

Toby, rejuvenated, turned back to feed Saaba when he spotted a green-robed giant heading into the woods. *Maybe, just maybe, we'll come out of this alive yet,* Toby thought.

An hour later the trolls were ready to move out. Blythar put the three "serving" trolls in charge of Toby, Saaba, and Deckor. "We'll let you walk unchained, but any attempt to escape will be met with immediate physical harm. We won't kill you. That's for Clygon to do. But you will wish you were dead after we're done with you. And as for your wolf, you can keep the muzzle off but if he attacks anyone, you will suffer the consequences, Hero! Make sure he knows that."

Blythar then looked admiringly at Saaba and said, "We lost four good trolls to your wolf when we captured you. It will take them months to heal up. Wish he was on our side!" And with that he walked away.

Toby and Deckor looked down at Saaba with renewed respect. Perhaps it was their imagination, but both were convinced Saaba gave them a mischievous grin.

As they started to walk Deckor said to the three trolls, "We are grateful for your hospitality. May we at least know your names?"

The trolls looked at each other and then at Deckor. They seemed genuinely shocked that he had asked such a question.

"I'm sorry if I have offended you or have asked a question that you are not permitted to answer."

Finally, one of the trolls spoke. "It's not that. We don't have names."

It was Toby's and Deckor's turn to looked at each other and then at the trolls. "What do you mean you don't have names?" Toby asked.

"We're triplets. I know. We don't look alike," said one of the trolls. "Our mom died while giving birth to us. Our father was away serving Clygon and lost his life during the war with the River Elves."

"I lost both of my parents in that same fight, what we call the Troll War," Deckor said softly. The three trolls and Deckor stared at each other, but not in hatred. They shared a mutual sorrow in that moment, all of them victims of war.

The troll continued. "The village moms shared the responsibility of caring for us but never gave us names. Only numbers. I'm #41. This is #42. And this is #43."

"Why those numbers?" asked Deckor.

"Because I'm orphan #41 in our village, and so on."

"We are Servant Trolls," #42 said. "We have no identity in our village. We are not allowed to fight as warriors. We cannot be leaders. We simply serve the needs of the camp or their prisoners." She—and yes, Toby was surprised to hear that she was a she—said this with a deep sense of sadness.

They walked for about a mile in silence when #43 spoke. "That smell back in the camp? What was it? Why did it cause the other trolls to choke? And why did it make us feel so… so… so…"

"Happy?" questioned #41.

"Content?" asked #42.

"Calm?" chimed in Toby.

"Yes, it was all of that and more. We've never, ever experienced feelings like that before."

"That was hope!" Deckor said. "It gives you the energy you need to keep on when everything seems all wrong. When it all seems broken. When it all seems, well, hopeless."

"Is hope real?" asked #42.

"It is," Toby answered. "It doesn't always fix things. But it forges faith in you so that you can keep moving ahead."

The three trolls nodded at them and then suddenly grew quiet and serious. Blythar was approaching.

"No talking to the trolls!"

"Sorry, sir," Deckor said. "We were just thanking them for taking such good care of us on behalf of the beneficent Clygon."

Beneficent? thought Toby. That's a big word. I'll have to ask Deckor what it means if I get the chance.

Blythar couldn't tell if Deckor was honoring his leader or dissing him, but he couldn't risk dismissing a compliment of Clygon or surely Clygon would hear about it.

"Hmmmffff!" he muttered. "And no talking to the prisoners," he barked at the three trolls. "We'll be taking a short break in a mile or so. No more talking!"

As he walked away Saaba growled at him. Blythar jumped and picked up his pace as he headed up to the front.

So as not to get #41, #42, and #43 into more trouble, they walked the next mile without speaking. Toby opened up his mind to the sounds of the forest and found they helped soothe him. While the feeling of hope continued to energize him, the anxiety of what was ahead started eating into his imagination.

Something suddenly fell from the sky, hitting Toby on the head and landing at Deckor's feet. The three trolls quickly looked around, trying to find its source. Deckor picked up the small rock and grinned at Toby. "See this little mark? It's Donold's mark! They must be tracking us!"

The trolls looked at him apprehensively and Deckor calmed them by putting a finger to his lips. "You are in no danger from us, friends. Let's say nothing about this to Blythar or Plythar."

One of the trolls behind them ambled up. "What's going on?" he demanded.

"Nothing, sir," said #41. "A small pinecone fell and hit this prisoner on the head. Unfortunately, it did no damage." The troll laughed and ambled back to his position with the other trolls bringing up the rear.

Toby hoped the troll had bought it, as these particular trees didn't grow pinecones.

A few minutes later the small band of trolls and their prisoners halted for a quick break. After a brief potty stop—*and wow is it hard to pee when someone's watching you*—the prisoners were given a few more cups of water and a piece of jerky. Then it was back on their feet and onto the trail to Clygon's stronghold.

This time Plythar joined them. "Would you like me to tell you what Clygon has in store for you, Hero?"

"No."

Deckor gave Toby a sharp look.

"Sorry. No thank you, sir," Toby mumbled.

Plythar laughed. "Your graciousness is much appreciated, Hero. I will honor your answer and will not spoil the fun for you. But I will give you a hint: You will never forget your time with Clygon! He'll have you in stitches, literally… if you live to tell about it!" With that, Plythar headed back to the front of the group, laughing the whole way.

Deckor turned to Toby and saw the fear in his eyes. "Don't let him get to you, Toby. He's trying to wear you down."

"He's doing a perfectly good job of it," Toby said.

They fell into another long period of quiet as Toby concentrated on putting one foot in front of the other. He counted steps for a while. He sang some songs in his head that matched the rhythm of his footsteps. One song in particular, wedged itself into his brain. Something about raindrops falling on his head.

Where did that song come from? He concentrated. He dived deep into his memory. He almost had it. *Spider-Man 2* with Toby Maguire! That's why the song was in his head! It was in *Spider-Man 2*!

He continued to hum the song to himself, adding in a word or two as he remembered them. Which ended up being just a word or two.

Then a memory stirred, metaphorically speaking, of his Grandma Baxter singing that song to him when he was younger. Apparently, it was a big hit back in the old days sung by one of Grandpa Baxter's favorite singers.

Once the song left him, he imagined eating a big, huge, juicy burger slathered in ketchup, mustard, onions, and BBQ sauce. And then his mind went numb.

Just when he felt like his legs were about to fall off, he heard a rustling in the trees to his left. The trolls heard it as well. The march halted. The trolls looked around nervously, poised for an attack. "Just the wind!" he heard one of the trolls behind him shout.

They resumed their march. But Toby noticed Deckor glancing from side to side. The movement of his head was slight but Toby could tell that he was looking for something. Saaba, too, seemed on high alert. #'s 41, 42, and 43 could feel the tension and looked at Deckor. He nodded his head to them slightly. And then he tripped. He fell to his knees and caught himself with his hands.

"Duck!" he whispered as loudly as he could to Toby.

Toby looked up, expecting to see a duck.

"He means get down!" #42 whispered quickly.

Did I just fall into a Homonym? A Homonym? What in the world is a Homonym and what is going on in my brain? He'd have to Google it when he got home.

As soon as Toby hit the ground the arrows started flying. #'s 41, 42, and 43 formed a circle around Toby and Deckor and quickly led them into the woods, off the path. They heard trolls screaming in pain and others yelling orders. Saaba was howling and growling and from the sounds of it, tearing into troll legs with his sharp teeth.

They were able to peak out from the woods and saw mass chaos. Arrows continued to fly into the trolls. Saaba was running after Plythar, who was running from Saaba in a panic.

Then Toby saw Donold running with his sword toward two trolls. Coming from the other side was Johanna, along with Mathilda. Judah came from yet another direction yelling at the top of his lungs with Clovor at his side.

Deckor moved to join them but #41 held him back. "You have no weapon. You are safer here." Deckor didn't like it but he did as he was told.

The trolls who were still able to stand and fight—about 10 of them, Toby counted—formed a circle with their backs to each other. Clovor, Mathilda, Donold, Judah, Phoenix, Johanna, and Saaba surrounded the trolls, facing them, with the Healer a ways off to the side.

"Drop your weapons and you will live!" shouted Clovor.

"Don't do it, trolls. We fight for Clygon. We will not give in to these River Rats." It was Blythar.

"One last chance!"

"We will never surrender to you!" Blythar yelled.

But Blythar was smiling.

Why is he smiling?

The River Elves began to advance on the circle of trolls when Mathilda cried out and fell to the ground. And then Judah fell. Clovor and Donold turned to see what had happened and Blythar and his trolls attacked. From out of the woods Toby could see twenty trolls running toward their fellow trolls and the River Elves. Saaba went onto the attack but suddenly he fell to the ground, an arrow in his side.

The battle lasted all of thirty seconds and the River Elves surrendered. Through the tears in his eyes Toby saw that both Judah and Mathilda had arrows in their thighs, but they were otherwise OK.

Suddenly Deckor ran out from the woods, yelling at the top of his lungs, but he didn't get far. A troll stepped into his path and hit him in the gut with the hilt of his sword, knocking the breath out of Deckor.

As Toby tried to take this all in, he heard a desperate whisper in his ear. It was #43. "Do as we say. Trust us. We will do our best to protect you."

"Where is the Hero?" Blythar yelled.

"We have him, sir," answered #41. "We had him the whole time. He was not going to get away. We knocked him out just to be sure."

"Huh?" Toby looked at #41.

"Bring him to me."

"I'm sorry, Toby. This will hurt but it will hopefully protect you." And with that, #41 sledge-hammered him on the head. And for the second time in two days Toby Baxter was knocked into la-la land by the fist of a troll.

CHAPTER 20

How Will You Use Your Power?

Toby woke up in a dark cell. It was cold. Something was sticking into his back and he realized it was damp straw. The place reeked of vomit, poop, urine, and some other nameless, horrific smells. A small barred window let in a bit of air and from the looks of it, it was night time.

He sat for a moment or two, rubbing his sore head. He was the proud owner of two huge bumps. If this is what #41 meant by saying this might save him, #41 was either wrong or had betrayed him.

He held his breath for a moment for two reasons: to try not to breathe in the putrid smells of the cell, and to see if he could hear anything that might give him a clue as to where he was.

And he did hear something. Breathing. In the cell. And it wasn't his breathing. He couldn't see anything so he carefully crawled along the floor, reaching out his hand. The cell was fairly big. Near the opposite wall he felt something soft. Feathers maybe? Whatever it was, it moved at Toby's touch. Then Toby heard the unmistakable shaking that confirmed his guess. His cellmate was Hiriam.

The Drone turned his head toward Toby.

"My good friend." Hiriam could barely get the words out. Apparently, it was too much work to maintain his human head and in a moment his bird head returned. Hiriam's deep breathing told him that Hiriam had passed out.

The door to his cell squeaked open. Two people entered, both holding torches.

"Toby, are you all right?" It was the Healer.

"Yes, I'm fine. But Hiriam's not. Can you check on him?"

The Healer quickly moved to Hiriam and began to slide his hands over the Drone's body. As he did so he started a low hum. Toby could feel its healing power in his own body.

The second person quietly placed a plate of food next to Toby, along with a cup of liquid.

"#41! What are you doing here?" Toby asked.

"How's your head?"

"Sore."

"I'm so sorry, Toby Baxter. I only had a moment to think and this seemed a better option than what Blythar would have done to you. I've snuck in some decent food for you and a cup of water. Blythar only ordered more of that rabbit broth. Eat up so I can get the plate and cup out of here before Blythar checks in on you."

As Toby ate, the Healer approached him. "I'm afraid Hiriam's right wing is broken and he's suffered a massive blow to his head. It looks like he might have taken an arrow to his side as well. I've done what I can for him. He needs rest."

"Where are the others?" Toby asked. "Are they safe? Are they all right? Did they manage to get away from the trolls?"

His questions were met with silence.

"Healer. Tell me. Where are the others? Are they OK?"

Still more silence.

Finally, the Healer answered. "Clovor, Phoenix, Deckor, Judah, Donold, and Johanna are here. They all bear wounds from their attempt to rescue you but none of them serious. Except for Saaba. His wound is angry and deep. They are being held in some of the cells in another part of this building…" His voice trailed off.

"Where's Mathilda? What are you not telling me?"

"We don't know where she is, Toby. She fell during the attack and we lost track of her."

"Is she alive? Can you tell me anything?"

Toby could see the Healer shake his head in the light of the torch. "We don't know, Toby. I've tried to find out but either the trolls I've spoken to don't know or won't tell me."

"Why are you here? Why are they letting you attend to us?"

"The trolls know that I am a Healer. They've allowed me to do what I can to fix you up, along with the rest of our group, as long as I attend to their own wounded first. Clygon wants you as strong as possible when you stand trial before him tomorrow."

"Trial? For what? What does he mean to do?"

Toby saw the Healer shudder. Toby shuddered, too.

They heard footsteps coming toward the cell. #41 quickly picked up the plate and the cup and hid them in his robe. He replaced them with a bowl filled with rabbit broth.

"Leave us!" boomed the voice of Blythar. #41 and the Healer left the cell, leaving Toby alone with a sleeping Hiriam and a vomit, sweat-smelling Blythar.

"What do you want now?" Toby shouted.

"Did you get enough to eat?" Blythar laughed.

Toby didn't answer.

Blythar sat down next to him. Toby had to hold back a gag.

"Tomorrow night you will finally get a chance to meet Clygon. He is anxious to welcome you to our home!" Another sickening laugh. "You will want to rest up. The fate of your friends rests on you, Hero!"

Blythar stood up, walked to the door, and laughed one more time. "See you tomorrow, Hero!"

And with that he slammed the cell door and locked it.

Toby sat in the silence listening to Hiriam's breathing. He felt tears of anger and fear welling up in his eyes but he fought them back. Clovor would be upset with him but he didn't need tears right now. He needed a strategy. Yet, try as he might, he couldn't come up with anything. And it was hard to think, as he was consumed with worry over his friends, especially Mathilda.

Toby!

Toby!

He must have fallen asleep. Then again, maybe he was still sleeping. It was so dark he couldn't tell.

Toby!

It was the voice of his grandpa. But the smell of Christmas suggested that it was the Christmas Giant speaking to him, using the voice of his grandpa. He felt a deep sense of calm wash over him.

Toby, tomorrow you will be required to show yourself a man… to show yourself a Hero.

"What does that mean? I keep telling everyone, I'm just a kid! I'm only thirteen. I've never done anything heroic in my life!"

Heroes are made in the small moments of life, Toby. Those small moments prepare you for those big moments when you are called upon to do something you don't believe you can do. Those small moments, added up, shape you into a heroic man.

"I have no idea what you are talking about!"

Think, Toby! Remember two weeks ago at school during that big math test?

"I got stuck on one of the questions."

Right. As Clarissa worked on the test, she moved her arm just enough and you could see her answers. And what did you do?

"I… um… I quickly looked back at my own test paper so as not to cheat."

Exactly. You acted Honorably in that moment. And there have been many moments like that in your life this past year. They add up. And how about that time a month ago when your mom took your iPad away for a week?

"What was so heroic about that? I got into trouble."

But what did you learn?

Toby thought.

Come on, Toby, what did you learn?

"I could use a bit more of that Christmas smell about now!"

In a moment. Think Toby. What did you learn?

"That I need to be more involved with real life… to get out of the sometimes-mind-numbing zone of technology and find creative ways to engage with life?"

Yes, and you made a commitment to yourself to use your iPad wisely, not allowing it to distract you from your family or friends.

Toby got a new whiff of hope. He could feel an increasing sense of confidence.

What about that time a month ago when your friend Benny was picking on that new kid at your school, and your friends were egging him on?

"I told him to leave the kid alone, I guess."

You guess? You were the only one to stick up for the little guy. And what happened?

"Benny and some of my friends stopped hanging with me and started hanging with Derrick!"

You paid a price for doing the right thing. Would you do it again?

Toby hesitated then said, "Yes! Of course I'd do it again."

Toby waited for the Giant to say more. But the Giant fell silent.

After several moments Toby said, "It's too much. I don't know what to do."

Tomorrow, Toby, you will be put to the test. How will you use your power? How will you use your unique gifts and talents when you come face to face with Clygon? Will you give in to your anger and hatred? Will you give into despair? Will you choose violence? Or will you find an answer to the greatest challenge you have faced so far, Toby, and show yourself to be a Hero? How will you use your power?

Toby sighed. "I have no idea."

Toby, dig into your pocket.

Toby stuck his hand into his pocket and pulled out the ancient compass. He'd forgotten all about it.

That compass will guide you, Toby, when your moment comes.

Toby remembered the talk with his dad at *Dairy Queen* and the small card with the compass on it his dad had given to him:

Honorable—Do the right thing. Always.

Enterprising—Find a way forward.

Responsible— Use your gifts and abilities in the service of others.

Original—Be yourself.

I will leave you with this, Toby. You will be faced with a difficult choice. You will be tempted by violence to use violence. You will be tempted by despair to give in to despair. You will be tempted by hatred to respond in kind. But tomorrow you can draw a line in the sand and show Clygon what kind of man you are going to be. Be a Hero, Toby! I believe in you.

Toby woke up. Sunlight was shining through the small window in the cell. He could see Hiriam, still sleeping, his breathing deep and even. Hopefully he was healing. But then again, what was the point of healing today?

And yet, just as despair was about to engulf him, Toby smelled Christmas again. He looked up and saw a huge, bearded face in the barred window. The face smiled at him.

I believe in you, Toby! Show yourself to be a man!

It was the voice of his grandpa.

CHAPTER 21

Clygon!

Toby slept on and off all day long. #41 brought him some food and water. The Healer stopped by and seemed pleased with Hiriam's healing, although Hiriam had slept all day.

"Any word on Mathilda?"

"Nothing." The Healer didn't expand on his answer.

"Toby, let me see your right hand."

Toby showed the Healer his right hand and the green mark Grandpa had put there.

"Remember, Toby Baxter. You are not alone."

The Healer headed back out of the cell, leaving Toby with a sleeping Hiriam.

Just when he thought he would go mad the cell door swung open.

"On your feet, Hero!" Blythar commanded.

"You, too, Drone!" It was Plythar.

Hiriam didn't respond so Plythar kicked him.

Toby rushed Plythar and managed to give him a good kick in the groin. Toby then quickly moved to the wall, his back facing it, ready to protect himself. Ready to fight.

When Plythar was able to breathe again he walked over and slapped Toby across the face with the back of his hand. Tears immediately came to Toby's eyes and Plythar laughed. Toby really, really hated that laugh. He couldn't wait to wipe that smug look from Plythar's face.

Blythar forced a stunned Hiriam to his feet, put a chain around the Drone's neck, and dragged him limping out of the cell.

Plythar grabbed Toby by the arm in a vice-like grip and pushed him out the cell door.

They walked down a long, dark corridor lit by flaming torches. Occasionally they could hear screaming from the cells. *Was the screaming coming from his friends?* His rage grew.

They ascended what seemed like two-hundred stairs before coming out into the fresh air, if that's what you call vomit and sweat-filled air.

Toby was marched to an open area with flaming torches planted in enough places so as to light up the field. Loud boos met him. Hundreds of trolls sat in bleachers surrounding the field. It felt like being in a gladiator movie.

Blythar chained Hiriam to a tree stump off to the left of Toby. The Drone collapsed into a heap, exhausted by the journey from the cell to the field.

Suddenly the booing and hissing and taunting stopped. Everything fell still. Toby tried to move but Plythar's grip was too strong.

A movement to his right caught Toby's eye. All of the trolls looked that way as well. They rose to their feet. Then erupted into chanting:

"*Cly-gon! Cly-gon! Cly-gon! Cly-gon!*"

Surrounded by four guards, with #41, #42, and #43 following behind, strutted an obese, wrinkled, hairless troll, about the same height as Toby.

He had an enlarged nose with a huge bump—wart?—on the end of it. His ears were rippled with blood veins. With each step the blubber on the troll wiggled and shimmied through his fur robe. It was disgusting.

The troll stopped and looked straight at Toby. Toby had experienced many frightening moments in this world. But looking into the eyes of Clygon made his bowels squirm and his stomach churn. He wanted to vomit, among other things. This was no fat slob troll. This troll had power.

Clygon smiled at Toby, sending chills deeper into his intestines.

"Where are you, Christmas Elf?" Toby whispered.

Clygon's procession led to what looked to be a throne in the middle of the bleachers. As he took a seat so did the rest of the trolls, and the cheering stopped.

It was then that Toby saw it. Lying between him and the bleachers. Still locked in cement fragments. The Sword. His Sword, apparently. Looking at it, Toby felt a surge of electricity run up and down his spine.

Clygon saw him looking at the Sword and laughed. A deep, vulgar, sickening laugh.

"Not much use to you now, is it, Toby Baxter?" The trolls erupted into cheers.

Toby despised them all. Looking at Clygon he felt the rage welling up in him. Clygon seemed pleased to see it. In fact, Clygon seemed to feed off of it.

"I thought you might like some company, Toby Baxter!" Clygon waved his hand.

To his left Toby saw two guards leading out a group chained to each other. Toby tried not to gasp but couldn't help himself.

The guards led Clovor, Phoenix, Deckor, Judah, Johanna, Donold, and Saaba out onto the field next to Hiriam. They all had bruises on their faces. Their clothes were torn. Deckor, Judah, and Donold were limping. Saaba was on some sort of hammock, pulled across the ground by a guard.

The wolf looked at Toby and Toby could feel the wolf's pain. The Healer was with them but not chained to the rest. Apparently, he still had the freedom to attend to the wounded. But again, why would that matter now?

Toby heard a squawk and saw a Drone land next to Clygon. It had to be the traitor, Demetrius. It put on its human head and spoke.

"Well, well, well. Greetings to my good friends, the River Elves."

I'll wipe that pompous look off of that Drone's face! Toby promised quietly.

Demetrius looked at Toby and smiled. A big, almost friendly smile. "So nice to finally make your acquaintance, young Toby Baxter. I knew your great-grandfather. I knew your grandfather. And I knew your father. I suspect you will prove to be just as weak and disappointing as they were."

The trolls rose up in a chorus of laughter. Even Clygon rose to his feet, laughing with them. But Toby wasn't laughing. He was fuming. He could feel the anger-driven power growing in him. He looked at the Sword and saw something no one else saw. It moved. It moved toward Toby.

At the same time, he saw Clygon shift and change. It seemed that the angrier Toby became, the more sleek, muscled and buff Clygon became. Clygon was growing in power, fueled by Toby's rage.

Violence met with violence only creates more violence.

Clygon sat down. The trolls followed.

"You seem angry, Toby Baxter. Tsk. Tsk. Tsk. Didn't your mom or that pathetic man you call your dad ever teach you to count to ten?"

More laughter from the trolls. More rage in Toby. He could tell Clovor was trying to get his attention, but he ignored her.

Clygon motioned the crowd with his hand and all fell silent. He stood up.

"Toby Baxter, I have a present for you."

Clygon nodded his head and two more trolls walked onto the field carrying what looked like a large blanket between them. Something was rolled up inside of it.

The two trolls held the blanket by the edges then threw it out, spilling its contents onto the ground. At first Toby couldn't see what it was. But then Judah cried out, "Mathilda!"

She lay lifeless on the grass. Blood streaked her hair and face. The Healer ran to her and checked her pulse. He looked up at Toby, his face grim. "She's barely alive," he whispered and immediately started to sing healing to her. Toby heard Clovor begin to weep. He turned and saw Donold fighting desperately to free himself, only to be knocked in his temple by a sword butt from one of the troll guards.

It was too much. Toby broke. He fell to his knees. He wept. His whole body gave way to grief and despair. It was useless. He was just a kid. He had no super powers. He was no Hero! The more Toby sobbed, the deeper his sense of powerlessness, the more the trolls cheered. Toby knew it was over. He'd failed. He'd let his friends down.

Clygon laughed at him. "Just like your dad! And your grandpa! And your great-grandpa! Weak. Useless. And because of you, Toby Baxter, your friends will die!"

And with that, Toby Baxter snapped. Rage, anger, hatred, and violence exploded out of him in a primal yell. He jumped to his feet. As he did so he reached out his right hand and the Sword sprang to life. It shattered its way out of the concrete and landed in Toby's right hand. A dark blood-red glow surrounded him. Plythar was thrown several feet away by the power surge.

"Toby! Toby! Don't give in! Look at him, Toby! Look at Clygon! He wants you angry. He's feeding off of your anger. Toby! Look at me! Please! Look at us!" Judah shouted until he was hoarse.

How will you use your power?

"Because of you your friends will die!"

Show yourself to be a man!

"You're just like your dad! Weak!"

I believe in you!

Toby felt power flowing from him into the Sword. He had to hold onto the hilt with both hands to steady it. Rage, hatred, and despair collided in his mind. He could see that Clygon wanted him enraged. He needed Toby to meet his violence with violence in order to defeat Toby and the River Elves once and for all.

Toby could hear wind swirling around him. It was almost deafening. Clygon continued to grow in power. Clygon was enjoying this.

Toby's friends yelled for his attention. His friends wanted something from him that he couldn't give.

Then he felt something buzzing in his pocket. The compass! Hanging on to the Sword as best he could with his right hand, he stuck his left hand into his left pocket, pulled out the compass, and looked at it. The arrow was spinning wildly…

… He found himself in the school lunchroom carrying his lunch tray over to the table where his friends were waiting for him. Walking a few steps behind him was the new kid, Sid. They'd not yet met. Suddenly a chair slid out in front of Toby, causing him to trip. He landed flat on the floor with a loud crash, spilling his lunch. Sid couldn't stop in time and tripped over Toby, his lunch splashing all over Toby. The entire lunchroom erupted into applause. Looking over, Toby saw Derrick and Derrick's friends laughing. It was Derrick who had pushed the chair out in front of him…

Toby felt his anger deepen. He felt his power grow. As he stared at Clygon he saw the face of Derrick.

Two troll guards tried to rush Toby but he flicked the Sword, sending both of the trolls flying backwards, landing hard on the ground. It felt so good. Like that moment when he had held the dagger to the troll's throat at the gnome village.

Clygon, feeding off of that anger, continued to grow in mass and size.

The compass buzzed again. The arrow stopped.

Honorable

… Now back in the lunchroom he slowly peeled himself up off the floor, covered in his lunch. Derrick and his friends continued to laugh at Toby and Sid while the janitor headed over to clean up the mess. Toby faced Derrick, his hands clenched at his sides. He was so angry and embarrassed he could feel tears starting to well up in his eyes. He took a step toward Derrick, when Sid stepped in front of him. Sid winked at Toby and then turned to Derrick with a big smile. He leaned over the table to Derrick and reached out his mayonnaise-covered hand, inviting Derrick to shake it. The entire lunchroom went silent as Sid stood there with a big, dopey grin on his face, his hand outstretched. Derrick, sensing everyone was watching, slowly shook hands with Sid, who said to Derrick, "Hey, friend. My name is Sid. I'm new here. I'm… we're…"—he nodded toward Toby—"sorry about the mess." With that Sid knelt down to help the janitor clean up the lunch on the floor. Toby, his fists still balled up in anger, watched as Derrick and his buddies slinked out of the lunchroom. They couldn't get out of there fast enough…

Toby's fist tightened on the Sword. As his hatred toward Clygon grew, the glow around him turned increasingly fire red.

Clygon shut his eyes. He leaned his head back and opened his arms, taking in Toby's rage. From deep inside, a loud laughter burst out of Clygon. A bone-chilling laughter.

From somewhere in the distance Toby heard someone yelling his name. But he ignored it.

The compass was buzzing so furiously that it had heated up to the point of being hot to the touch. Toby was forced to look at it.

Enterprising

... Now Toby was on the floor next to Sid, cleaning up the mess.

"Why did you do that?" Toby asked Sid.

"Do what?"

"You know... shake Derrick's hand. He's the one who tripped us."

"I know. But what good would it do to get angry? My grandma is always telling me to meet meanness with kindness. I thought I would give it a try. I think it worked pretty well, don't you?" Sid slapped Toby on the back with a handful of mayonnaise...

As Toby's anger surged, another emotion followed it. Ugliness! It frightened him. He frightened himself. Was this the kind of person he was? Was this what it meant for him to be a Hero? Is this how he was supposed to use his super powers, whatever they were?

In the midst of the wind and the anger and the taunting by the trolls, a surprising calm hit him. He could smell Christmas.

Clygon's eyes flew open. Did Clygon smell it, too? He looked down at Toby, his confidence wavering. Toby could see it.

Toby looked back at the compass.

Responsible

... Now he was sitting in youth group at church, his new friend Sid next to him. The youth leader was explaining an odd Bible passage to them. Something about heaping burning coals on someone's head. It didn't seem very Biblical.

"Sounds like something we should do to Derrick," Toby whispered to Sid. They both laughed.

"Turns out," the youth leader said, "the verse is an invitation to treat your enemy with kindness."

"Doesn't sound like it," Toby whispered to Sid.

"A few lines earlier," the youth leader went on, "the writer says: *'Repay no one evil for evil, but give thought to do what is honorable in the sight of all.'*

"To heap burning coals on the head of your enemy is to draw a line in the sand," the youth leader continued. "To treat him with kindness. To respond to her anger with grace. To treat that person like a valued human-being. And hopefully, that will re-ignite the flame of his or her own conscience."

"That's what you did to Derrick last month!" Toby said to Sid…

Toby took in another large whiff of Christmas. Clygon's eyes widened in horror.

The compass buzzed.

Original

… Now Toby Baxter was back at *Dairy Queen,* watching as his dad handed Derrick that $20 bill and the confusion on Derrick's face at his dad's act of kindness.

Toby saw it then. Dad met Derrick's meanness toward Toby with kindness. *Your friend doesn't know what hit him,* Toby remembered his dad saying…

Toby felt his anger subsiding. He wasn't a warrior. At least not a hand-to-hand-in-combat kind of warrior. He didn't have those kinds of fighting skills. Was there another way to defeat Clygon?

As his own rage retreated, Clygon's power seemed to wane as well.

You can draw a line in the sand…

Toby put the compass back into his pocket, once again grabbing the hilt of the Sword with both hands. The glow around Toby began to grow again, turning from fire-red to sunshine-yellow. He looked Clygon in the eyes. And smiled.

Clygon began to scream. "No! Stop him! Stop him before it's too late."

"Anyone who wants to stand for peace, anyone who wants this battle between the trolls and River Elves to end, come to me!" Toby shouted through the hurricane engulfing him.

No one moved. At first.

But then, #41, #42, and #43 ran over to Toby and stood behind him. The guards watching the River Elves joined him. Fifty Trolls ran from the stands to Toby. And then another fifty.

All the while Clygon was yelling: "No! Stop him."

"Clygon!" Toby shouted. "Join us! It's time for this animosity between the trolls and the River Elves to end!" But Clygon continued to yell and scream at his guards to stop Toby.

In the midst of the rushing wind and the noise and the energy, a voice called out: "Demetrius! Come!" Toby looked over to see Hiriam leaning on Clovor, his eyes pleading with Demetrius. "Demetrius! Friend! Come!"

Demetrius's eyes went wild. He looked at Clygon and then back at Hiriam, unsure what to do. But something in the voice of Hiriam compelled Demetrius to fly off the bleachers to the River Elves. Hiriam had called him Friend.

Finally, Plythar acted. He pulled out his sword and began to rush Toby. He was too late.

Toby radiated an energy that worked like a force field. It repelled Plythar's attack, throwing him backwards onto the ground. Clygon was now back to his old blubbery self. He watched, paralyzed by what was about to happen, as Toby lifted his Sword, and then turned it around, the tip of the Sword facing the ground, the hilt in the air. Both of his hands encased the hilt, now raised above his head.

Show yourself to be a man!

Draw a line in the sand!

You are not alone!

I believe in you, Toby!

Clygon's eyes, now big as saucers, took in the full horror of what was about to happen.

Toby Baxter, glowing with energy, glowing with hope, plunged the Sword into the ground at his feet. As he did so, light exploded out of the ground. The earth cracked beneath his feet. He heard Clygon shouting… cursing… He heard the trolls on the bleachers screaming and running.

He heard Mathilda shouting. "Toby!"

Then it all went dark.

CHAPTER 22

Wait! What Just Happened?

Toby sat up. He was in a bed. The room was dark. He had no idea where he was. As his eyes began to adjust, he realized that he was in his own bed in his own bedroom. He grabbed the iPad sitting on the lamp stand. It was 3 a.m. *The early morning after his birthday!*

Toby was absolutely discombobulated. *Discombobulated?* Another big word. He quickly looked it up on Dictionary.com:

Discombobulated
To confuse or disconcert; upset; frustrate

Once his head cleared and he'd got his bearings, he jumped out of bed and ran into the closet. He immediately found himself outside in bright sunshine—the waterfall to his right, the stone wall behind him, the stream in front of him, and the small bridge to the path on the other side of the stream a few feet away. He ran over the bridge and stopped to look up the hill in front of him. The stone that had once held the Sword, destroyed by the trolls, had been repaired. Toby could see the cracks in it. The Sword, however, was not there.

Toby took off down the path to *RiverHome*. In a matter of seconds he had to stop. The little stones and debris on the path were cutting into his feet. He had no shoes on! And to his embarrassment he found he was wearing *Iron Man* pajamas. Where had his elven leathers gone?

He walked as quickly as his feet would allow. Thankfully the path was covered by fallen leaves, making the path somewhat manageable, although the little stones hurt. He looked up. The trees were almost bare. How did that happen? It was summer here, wasn't it?

As he rounded the corner the playing field came into view. It looked like a big carnival or circus had come to the village. The field was crowded with tents, animals, elves, gnomes, and trolls. *Trolls?*

The path was empty. Everyone was apparently at the carnival. He headed for Grandpa's and Grandma's home. Before he could get there, however, someone grabbed him from behind, twisted him around, and gave him a great big bear hug, the hugger's head coming up to Toby's chest. The hugger was joined by another, and then another.

"You're… squeezing… me… too… hard!" Toby squeaked out.

Clovor, Deckor, and Judah let go of him only for another elf to attempt to hug him nearly to death. It was Phoenix.

"Grandma had a sense that you would be coming today!" said Phoenix. "We've been on the lookout since breakfast."

Toby heard whimpering behind him. He turned around to see Jerry coming toward him, with Saaba following behind him. Saaba's hind leg was in some sort of a sling attached to a wheel, enabling him to walk on three of his legs. The device didn't seem to bother him as he darted for Toby, and to the best of his ability, jumped up onto him, almost licking his face off.

"Toby, why are you in your pajamas? Why don't you have shoes on? Where have you been?" The questions poured out of Clovor. "Never mind for now. Let's get you to the house, clean you up, feed you, and get you some real clothes. Then we can chat."

Clovor, Deckor, Judah, Phoenix, Jerry, and Saaba led Toby down the path to Grandpa's house. They entered the now familiar hole that led into the home. Toby ducked his head and then straightened up again when they entered the huge hall.

Grandpa was there to greet him. The elderly elf took both of Toby's hands into his. He rubbed his thumb along the green mark on Toby's right hand. He looked up into Toby's eyes, his eyes filled with tears, and he said, "Bless you, my son. You brought them home!" He let go of Toby's hands and then bowed to him.

Toby had no idea what to do. But it didn't matter, because Grandma saved the moment. She hugged him and said, "Come in, Toby. Come in! Let's get you out of those pajamas and into some clothes. And let's get a pair of shoes on your feet. Judah, can you help Toby find something to wear? We'll get the food ready for you."

Judah led Toby down the hallway to Toby's *RiverHome* bedroom. Judah pulled some leathers out of one of the dresser drawers and found a pair of elven boots. He playfully punched Toby in the stomach and said, "It's good to see you again, Toby." He left the room to give Toby some privacy.

Toby quickly dressed and then sat down on the bed to catch his breath. All kinds of questions swirled around in his brain as he tried to make some sense of what was going on.

He was brought back into the moment by a knock on the door. "May I come in?" It was Clovor.

"Yes! Please!"

Clovor entered the room and sat down next to Toby. She put her arm around his waist and sat silently with him for several moments.

"You saved us, Toby Baxter," she finally said.

"How? What happened? How long have I been gone? Is the troll threat over? What happened to the Sword? And where's Mathilda?"

As if on cue Mathilda burst into the room and threw herself at Toby, knocking him off the bed and landing on top of him. She hugged him as best she could, laughing and giggling uncontrollably. "You're back! Toby! You're back! I thought we'd lost you." Then she stood up, held out her hand, lifted Toby to his feet, and promptly punched him in the chest. "Where have you been, Toby Baxter! We... thought... we'd... lost... you," she said, now through tears. She hugged him again.

"Mathilda, how about we fill in all the blanks over dinner. Come, let's join the others." Clovor led them down the hallway to the main hall. Others had filed into the house by then: Donold, Johanna, the Healer, Victor, and Ethol. Jerry was there with Saaba. In the corner, snuggling Phoenix, was Roxie, with Saanti the wolf sitting next to them. Toby noticed that Saanti no longer growled at Phoenix, so apparently something good was going on between Phoenix and Roxie.

Toby heard a familiar squawk, followed by the sound of a large bird shaking its head. Hiriam was up on his perch. Seated next to him was Demetrius. Hiriam bowed his head to Toby. Demetrius looked embarrassed to be there.

At Grandpa's direction everyone took a seat around the table. Toby sat between Clovor and Deckor. Saaba walked/wheeled himself over and squeezed in between Deckor and Toby, and then awkwardly lied down. *Or is it laid down? Mrs Grayson would be very disappointed in his command of certain aspects of English grammar.*

Grandpa motioned for quiet. He held up a goblet. "To the Creator, the Author of this bounty!" The guests held up their goblets and repeated, "To the Creator, the Author of this bounty!"

"And to Toby Baxter, our Hero!"

"To Toby Baxter, our Hero!"

Toby's face turned bright red as he, along with the others, took a big gulp of that delicious, energizing elven juice... draught... drink... tonic... whatever it was.

The meal was, as usual, outstanding. Once in a while someone would ask him a question but the noise of the various conversations made it hard for Toby to answer. Clovor kept assuring him that after dinner they would answer all of his questions and he could answer theirs.

Once the dinner plates were cleared Grandma made an announcement: "I've been experimenting with various desserts for this moment when Toby would come back to us. I had a dream last night that today would be the day, Toby. So I've made this special dessert in your honor. I call it the *Hero's Delight*."

Grandpa walked out with a tray holding small, clear bowls. In each of them was something chocolate-looking. Grandpa set the first bowl down in front of Toby. His mouth watered as he looked at it but he politely waited until everyone had been served.

"I want you to be the first to try it, Toby," Grandma said. "And I want to see if you can tell me what's in it."

All eyes were on Toby. Once again he could feel his face turn red. He twirled the bowl around a few times. He noticed some sort of chocolate crumbs at the bottom, a chocolate-looking pudding, dark chocolate sauce, more chocolate crumbs on top, with some chocolate chips thrown in for extra measure.

He put a spoonful into his mouth, everyone eager for his reaction. Grandma stood next to him, holding her breath.

As the dessert hit his tongue an explosion of taste blew up in his mouth. Certainly chocolate—deep, rich, succulent chocolate—the best chocolate he had ever tasted. But more than that. His eyes filled with tears. And then he began to laugh. Uncontrollably. A deep, healing, belly laugh. A laugh that released all the tension and fear and anxiety that he had been holding in for so long. He was eating joy!

His laugh was contagious, and even before the others started in on their desserts, the whole room soon filled with uncontainable laughter and happiness.

Grandma looked on with a huge smile on her face.

Once the laughter died down, and it took a while, Grandma asked Toby to name the ingredients of the dessert.

"Elven magic! That's the best I can come up with. Elven magic, Grandma," answered Toby. "And thank you!"

Grandma, Grandpa, Clovor, and Judah cleared the table. Apparently, Grandma and Grandpa decided to allow others to help them out around the kitchen. Phoenix was busy whispering into Roxie's ear, holding her hand. Donold rekindled the fireplace. Mathilda grabbed Toby by the hand and led him outside. It was mid-afternoon. The carnival filled the sky with laughter, music, and the sounds of horses neighing.

"I thought you might like a bit of fresh air," Mathilda said.

They stood quietly together, enjoying the cool breeze.

"You saved my life, Toby! I'm grateful."

Toby didn't know what to say. He couldn't remember saving her life.

"It took me months to heal, Toby."

"Months?" Toby asked.

But Mathilda didn't hear him. "I was deeply scarred, physically and emotionally. Thank the Creator for the Healer. He put me back together. That... along with the help of a mutual friend."

Toby looked at her questioningly.

"The Christmas Elf," she whispered. "I saw him. Right before you disappeared. I knew then that I would live. Or at least I knew then that I wanted to live. That I *could* live. He gave me hope, Toby. Right as you disappeared."

Toby still didn't know what to say.

Deckor interrupted them. "They're ready!"

The three of them headed back into the house. The table had been moved up against the wall and a circle of chairs sat in the middle of the hall. Clovor invited Toby to sit next to her.

"Toby," Clovor said, and immediately she choked up. "Sorry, it's just that we're all so glad to see you. You've been gone for months!"

"Months?" Toby asked.

"What happened to you, Toby?" Donold asked

"I… I don't really know. I remember holding the Sword. I remember thrusting it into the ground. I remember some sort of explosion. And then I was in my bed in my room in my house. Moments later I ran back here!"

"Hmmmmm…" Clovor mumbled.

"Oh, and I remember Mathilda calling out to me just before I woke up in my bed. That's all I know. Sorry. What happened here?"

"As you know, we tried to rescue you from the trolls, but they had been waiting for us," Clovor began. "We thought we were ambushing them but it was a trap. They ambushed us. They took us to the Trolls' Stronghold. We were probably held down the hallway from where you and Hiriam were. They took Mathilda from us. We had no idea where she was or what had happened to her." Clovor had to pause to regain control of her emotions.

"That night they led us out onto the field where we saw you. And like you, we watched as they threw Mathilda onto the ground… broken."

The hall fell silent.

"We saw you start to glow. We saw the Sword fly to your hand. But I could tell there was something wrong. Clygon was feeding off of your anger. He was growing stronger. I tried to get your attention but you seemed unreachable. As we continued to watch, however, you changed. You seemed to realize that your anger was not serving you well. That it was Clygon's plan to drain you of your power by absorbing your anger."

"I saw things. I heard voices. I... I... the images, memories, voices... the compass..." he looked at Grandpa, "... showed me a better way," Toby tried to explain.

"Clygon could sense the change in you. So could we. Suddenly we felt hope. We willed you to keep going, Toby.

"And then you called for peace. You called the trolls to join us in peace. Some came. Clygon tried to stop you. And that's when you thrust the Sword into the ground, causing an explosion of light. You saved us in that moment, Toby."

"But how? What happened?"

"You drew a line in the sand. The Sword created a barrier between us and the trolls. For now, they cannot pass that barrier—that line in the sand. Unless their hearts speak peace. Somehow, the barrier knows. If a troll of peace moves toward the barrier, he or she is allowed to pass. But, if the troll intends to do us harm, the barrier stops him or her with a shock, like an electric fence."

"And how long will that hold?" Toby asked.

"We aren't quite sure," Judah answered. "What we do know is that we have not heard the last from him! Our intel tells us that he is trying to regain his power..." Judah shook his head in anger.

Clovor put a hand on his arm and smiled. "This is a time to celebrate, Cousin. We have nothing to worry about from Clygon today."

Judah smiled back and lifted his mug of elven ale. "To Toby Baxter!"

The rest lifted their mugs and replied, "To Toby Baxter!"

Mathilda sensed something in Toby. "What is it, Toby? What are you thinking?"

Toby was thinking that he didn't deserve their praise. "Well... none of it seems all that... heroic. Don't get me wrong, I'm glad that what I did has brought some peace and calm to *RiverHome*, but it doesn't seem all that... impressive."

"What do you mean, not heroic?" Mathilda challenged him.

"Well... um... I didn't really do anything. I didn't fight anyone or anything. I didn't engage in battle with the trolls. I didn't single-handedly defeat Clygon or his minions. I just stuck the Sword in the ground. What's so heroic about that?"

Mathilda walked over and punched him on the arm.

"Ow! What's that for?" Toby asked.

"You're a fool, Toby Baxter. You saved us, Toby! You saved me!" Mathilda had tears in her eyes.

"But... but... I just stuck the Sword in the ground," Toby whispered, mostly to himself. "I don't feel like a hero."

The room fell silent for a moment. Then Phoenix spoke up:

"It's a real conundrum!"

"A conun-what?" asked Toby.

He saw the collective eye rolls aimed at Phoenix.

"Never mind him, Toby," Judah said. "You can look it up later when you get back home!" He aimed a stink-eye at Phoenix who shrugged and snuggled back into Roxie.

"Toby," Donold interrupted. "I understand. I'm a warrior. I want to defeat my enemies in battle. But I've been trained for battle. I've been trained to fight. And I call on that training when necessary. You did the same thing. You called upon the resources you had—wise advice poured into you from people who love you, who teach you, people like your parents, your grandpa, elves like us. You did battle against Clygon with wisdom, Toby Baxter, and that wisdom defeated him, and brought peace to us."

"I suppose. But... it just doesn't seem all that... epic."

"Toby," Grandpa intervened. "You were in a life-or-death battle with Clygon. He almost broke you. And when he couldn't do that he tried to stir up hatred and anger in you. He wanted to feed off of it. The more your hatred grew the stronger he became. But Toby, you fought off that anger. You chose a different path. That is no small feat, my son. Heroes are made through the small choices they make each day to act honorably, to serve others, to build a better world. Once in a while those small choices aim toward something bigger. That's what happened for you. Face it, Toby Baxter, your choice to plant the Sword in the ground was a brave, wise act of heroism. Mathilda is right. You saved us."

"Where is the Sword now? Toby asked.

"Right where you put it," Phoenix answered, his arm still tightly wrapped around Roxie's shoulder. "It stands guard, as Clovor said, serving as the gatekeeper, so to speak, determining who is permitted to cross the line."

The group gave Toby a few moments to process what had happened.

Suddenly Mathilda stood up. "That's it, Toby Baxter. You're still not convinced. Come with me!"

"Where are we going?"

"To see what you've done, through what you call your seemingly unimpressive act of heroism."

She grabbed him by the hand and dragged him out of the house. The rest of the group followed. She led him across the bridge to the playing field and into the heart of the carnival. When the crowds saw Toby, they ran to him, cheering him.

Elves, gnomes, and trolls, cried out his name: *"To-by Bax-ter! To-by Bax-ter!"* Kids ran up to touch him. Elves hugged him. Gnomes tried to high-five him. Trolls looked at him in awe. Many had tears in their eyes.

"Thank you, Toby Baxter!"

"We love you, Toby Baxter!"

"You're our hero, Toby Baxter!"

Three trolls made their way through the crowd.

"#41! #42! #43!" Toby cried out. They all hugged him at once, nearly squeezing the air out of him.

"You look… you seem so… different!" Toby said.

"That's because of you, Toby," said #42. "You gave us our freedom!"

They hugged him again.

"We've chosen new names for ourselves, Toby, to mark our freedom. My name is now Prothar," said #41.

"Mine is Sythar," added #42.

"And mine is Thytar," #43 chimed in.

"We chose the names of heroes from our past—male and female trolls who lived honorably back before the Chaos," explained #41, now Prothar.

"And…" Prothar leaned close to Toby and whispered, "I chose Toby as my middle name!"

Before he could respond Toby heard a voice that made him seize up in terror. It was Blythar.

"Toby Baxter." Blythar bowed to Toby. "Can you forgive me? What you did… in that moment… something happened to me. Something happened to a lot of us trolls. We saw hate. And we saw peace. We chose peace. Because of you, Toby Baxter."

Toby stared at him. He felt someone moving his hand toward Blythar. Blythar took Toby's hand and shook it. And like Blythar, Toby saw peace.

"See," Mathilda whispered up to him. "That's what you did! Not so unimpressive after all, Hero!"

Before he could respond, #42/Sythar grabbed Toby by his hand and led him deeper into the carnival. Everywhere he went people cheered him or patted him on his back (truth be told, closer to his butt because of his height).

He spent the next several hours eating delicious carnival food, watching sword fights and feats of strength and mini-plays (one featuring a gnome "Toby Baxter" thrusting a sword into the ground), and riding on horses trained to go in a circle. He started to feel like a celebrity of sorts, though a reluctant one. Maybe he had done something heroic after all?

As the sun set, Deckor sought him out to bring him back to the house. By now Toby was exhausted and ready for bed.

Before he headed to his room, Deckor pulled him aside. "We don't know how much longer you have with us in *RiverHome*, but we have a surprise for you tomorrow. Early. At dawn. Sleep well."

CHAPTER 23

The Surprise

And sleep well he did. But it seemed as if he had just closed his eyes when he heard a knock at his door.

"Get dressed. It's time," Deckor said.

When he walked into the hall Grandpa, Grandma, Clovor, Phoenix, Deckor, Judah, and Mathilda were waiting for him.

Grandma threw her arms around his waist and held him for several moments. Then Grandpa grabbed Toby's hands in his. "Toby, it's time to say goodbye. In time you may forget us. But we will never forget you and what you've done for us. Go in the grace of the Creator." And for the last time, Grandpa bowed to Toby. Toby returned the act of honor with a bow of his own.

"Come. We don't have much time," Deckor said.

The cousins and Toby headed outside. It was still dark but dawn was beginning to break. All was quiet. They walked over the bridge to the playing field, empty except for a few tents.

Though the light was dim he could see that Phoenix was wearing a red jersey with the number 3 on it and *Palmer* written across the back of the shoulders.

"Carson Palmer was a great quarterback but didn't he fall one game short of the..."

Phoenix threw his hand over Toby's mouth. "Remember the Troll poop?" he whispered.

Judah shushed them.

They all looked around in anticipation.

"What are we waiting for?" Toby asked.

"Shhhhhhhh!" Mathilda hissed.

More silence as the dawn brought some much-needed light onto the field.

Then he heard something. It sounded like the flapping of bird wings, but on steroids. The trees began to blow and it felt like a helicopter was landing on top of them. Right before his eyes a huge flying dragon landed a few feet away. It was magnificent. Its scales the greenest green Toby had ever seen. A bright yellow stripe ran down its belly and under its tail. Its face was strangely beautiful.

It bent its head down, as if bowing to Toby.

"She wants you to move closer to her, Toby," Judah whispered.

Toby walked up so that he stood inches from the dragon's nose. He could feel its—her—warm breath cover his whole body. Her head alone was almost the size of Toby.

She brought her left wing around and enveloped him. He expected the wing to feel rough like sandpaper but it had a soft, leathery texture. It felt like a warm blanket. Toby leaned into the wing and tentatively reached out his hand to pet the dragon on her nose. As he did so the dragon closed her bright yellow eyes and let out a soft, gentle moan. Toby couldn't help himself. He began to weep. Not tears of sadness, but of profound gratitude for this deeply sacred moment.

The dragon slowly moved her wing back into place and opened her eyes. She licked Toby on the cheek—a sloppy, sticky kiss. She lifted her head and Toby rejoined the group. They watched as the dragon opened up her wings, leapt into the air, and soared into the sky.

Toby turned to thank his friends, only to be surprised yet again. Behind the cousins were three unicorns. They were as magnificent as Deckor had described them during their captivity in the troll camp—a lifetime ago. The three animals walked up to Toby and bowed their heads to him. He bowed his head to them in return. Then they took turns nuzzling him with their noses, careful not to spear him with their horns. Toby threw his arms around each of their necks and hugged them. His friends did the same.

They heard voices and the unicorns lifted their heads. It was time for them to go. They bowed one more time to the group, then turned, and with that, disappeared into the woods.

"Thank you!" Toby croaked out. That was all he could say. He felt something stir in his heart. Joy. But also sadness.

Something told him it was time to go home. His friends sensed it, too.

Without saying a word to each other, they all turned and walked toward the bridge. Once on the other side of the stream, they stopped.

"I need to go home," Toby said.

"We know," replied Clovor.

Clovor, Phoenix, Deckor, Judah, and Mathilda formed a circle around Toby and joined hands. They began to hum. The humming seeped deep into him. He could feel its energy growing in him, filling him with joy. With love. They were saying goodbye to him.

The humming lasted several minutes and then slowly died out. One by one the elves hugged him.

"I'll take him back to the portal," Deckor said.

Toby and Deckor walked slowly up the path toward the waterfall. Toby looked back one last time and waved to his friends. Then he rounded the corner, following behind Deckor, his friends gone from his view.

They crossed the small bridge over the stream, the spray from the waterfall covering them with mist.

Toby and Deckor looked at each other. There was nothing left to say.

"Thank you, Deckor. Thank you for everything."

"You're a good man, young Toby Baxter. We will not forget you."

Toby stepped through the portal. He turned back one more time but all he saw was the back wall of his closet.

CHAPTER 24

Grandma Baxter

"Knock! Knock! Knock! Toby, it's time to wake up, sleepy head. Grandma Baxter will be here in a few minutes with your birthday present. Breakfast is almost ready."

Toby picked up his iPad to check the time. 7 a.m. His mom had let him sleep in.

He jumped out of bed, threw on his *Spider-Man* bathrobe, ran his hand through his hair, and headed into the kitchen.

"Happy day-after-your-Birth…" His mom's voice trailed off and she stared at her son.

"Mom, what's wrong?"

"You… you… you look so different. Older. More mature. Like you grew up overnight! Even your pajamas don't seem to fit anymore."

Toby looked down and saw that his *Black Panther* pajamas had indeed gotten shorter in the legs and in the arms. Had they shrunk in the wash?

"You have to stop growing up so fast, Toby!" his mom said as she hugged him.

They were interrupted by the doorbell. Toby ran to the door and opened it. Grandma Baxter walked in carrying a big, long box with a bow on it.

"Is that for me?" Toby asked.

"Yes it is, honey, and hold your horses. You can open it after breakfast."

"Hey, mom," his dad said as he walked into the room. "Come on in. Jan's in the kitchen. Breakfast is ready."

After giving thanks for the meal, they dove into waffles, eggs, bacon, and fresh squeezed orange juice. Grandma Baxter asked Toby about yesterday's birthday party and he told her about the gift cards he'd received and the fun they'd had. He gave a few details on what he was learning in school and Grandma Baxter shared some stories about when Toby was a little boy.

"Mom, if I promise to help clean up the dishes later, can we go into the living room and open the present from Grandma Baxter?"

"Of course. I'm sure I couldn't make you wait anyway."

They took their places in the living room and Grandma Baxter handed Toby the big, long box with the bow on it. As he reached out to grab the box his mom asked, "Toby, what's that green line on your hand?"

"Um... ah... well... um..."

"Your father used to have one just like that when we were dating. It was pretty faded but you could still tell it was there. It eventually disappeared. And now you have a bright green one. It wasn't there yesterday. Where did you get it?"

His dad was looking at his hand. "I had a mark like that?" But a memory was stirring.

Grandma Baxter interrupted. "Toby, this gift is from your Grandpa Baxter. He wanted this to be given to you when you turned thirteen."

"What is it?" Toby asked.

Grandma Baxter laughed. "Open it and find out!"

Toby removed the bow and then ripped off the tape that held the box closed. When he finally got the box open, he gasped. It was the Sword! The same Sword he'd used to stop Clygon. *How did it get here?*

He held it up with his right hand. He could feel its power. He could feel its energy. And then he noticed writing on it: *Loach*.

"*Low—ache?*" Is that how you pronounce it? Toby asked.

"It's *Lay-uk*. It's Celtic for Hero," Grandma Baxter said. "It's the name of the Sword!"

Suddenly his dad stood up and raced off toward the basement.

"What's that about, I wonder?" his mom asked.

"I think he's remembered something," Grandma Baxter said.

His dad came running back up with a box identical to the one Toby had just opened. But the box was empty.

"When I turned thirteen my Grandpa Baxter gave me a Sword just like that one. I'd forgotten all about it. But it seems to be missing."

"Oh, it's not missing, Thomas. This is that very Sword. Your father took it several years ago to give to Toby. Jan, you remember, don't you? Grandpa was pretty sick by that time and he asked if he could go into your basement to grab something for Toby."

Toby's mom nodded, but had no idea what was going on.

"But why? Why not just buy him a new one?" his dad asked.

"Give him your Sword, Toby," Grandma Baxter said.

Toby handed the Sword to his father, and as his dad took it into his hand, his eyes widened. "Oh!" And then again: "Oh!" Toby could see that his dad felt the energy of the Sword.

Then his dad looked at him, his eyes wide with wonder. "Clovor? Phoenix? Deckor? Judah? Mathilda? *RiverHome?*"

"Yup!" Toby said.

"What are you talking about, Thomas? Who are Clovor, Phoenix and whatever other names you mentioned? And *River House?* What is that? Where is that?"

Toby felt badly for his mom. She was obviously discombobulated.

"Jan, honey," his dad said. "I... just remembered that... I have... a special thingy that I... uh... planned... um... today, for Toby. We need to be there ASAP."

"What thingy?" Toby's mom asked. "This is the first I'm hearing about it."

"Jan," Grandma Baxter said. "It's OK. They have a lot to talk about, I think."

"About what?" Jan asked. "What's going on?"

"I'll fill you in in a moment. Now, you boys go and enjoy that thingy. I'm guessing you have lots of stories to tell."

"Grandma Baxter, do you know?" Toby asked her.

"I do, dear. Your grandfather told me all about it just before he died. He'd forgotten *RiverHome,* but apparently someone or something brought the memories back to him around the time he found out he was very sick. The more he remembered, the brighter the green mark on his hand became. I'm excited to hear your story, Toby, and yours, too, Thomas. But first I'll let the two of you go and do your thingy!" Grandma Baxter kissed Toby on the cheek.

Toby stood up to go but then turned back to Grandma Baxter. "Grandpa guided me through *RiverHome.* I heard him. He talked to me." Grandma Baxter's eyes filled with tears, and she smiled.

With that Toby ran into his bedroom and threw on some clothes. Then he and his dad hopped into the car and headed down to the lake for a long walk and a long talk.

Epilogue

Toby closed *The Hobbit*, feeling a sense of great satisfaction. He'd actually just finished reading an entire book from cover to cover. It took him several weeks, but he did it. He put the book onto the nightstand, turned off the light, and promptly fell asleep.

In his dream someone was shaking his foot. Someone was trying to wake him up. Someone was calling his name.

"Toby!" the voice whispered. "Toby, are you awake?"

Toby opened his eyes. It wasn't a dream. At the foot of his bed stood Author, glowing, reading glasses hanging around his neck, the pencil tucked into the top of his ear, and the notebook in his hand. He was wearing the same clothes but this time a Minnesota Twins baseball cap covered his bald head.

"Hey!" Toby said, trying to wake up his brain.

"Hey!" Author replied back, a beaming smile on his face.

Author took the pencil from his ear, put on his reading glasses, opened up his notebook, and sat down on the foot of the bed. "You've been on quite an adventure, my friend."

"Ya think?" Toby laughed.

"But it's not quite done yet."

"It's not?" Toby wasn't sure if he should be excited or wary.

"No, it's not," said Author. "Every good story needs an Epilogue."

"A what?"

"An Epilogue," Author answered. "An Epilogue wraps up a story. It ties up any loose storylines. It helps the reader feel complete. Or sometimes it leaves the reader with a cliffhanger, suggesting that another story might be ahead."

"O… K…" Toby said hesitantly.

"I've noticed that you're not looking above my head reading my words, so you're still into the story. That's good," Author observed, "but it also means that we need to wrap up this part of your story."

"O… K…" Toby said hesitantly, again. "How?"

"It depends," Author said.

"On what?"

"On the Epilogue. Will your Epilogue bring an end to your adventures in *RiverHome* or set up a new one?"

"Ummm… how do I know if it's an ending or a beginning?"

"You get to decide. Any ideas?"

Toby stared at him blankly, still not fully awake.

"Well… Would you like to go back to *RiverHome?*"

"Really?" Toby asked. "I can go back?"

"I don't see why not," Author answered. "I think your friends would like to see you again."

Toby frowned. "Is something wrong? Are they in trouble?"

Author made a note but didn't say anything.

"Tell me!" Toby said. "Are they in trouble?"

More silence.

"OK. I get what you're doing here. You're trying to set up a cliffhanger, right?"

Author smiled.

Toby rubbed his tired eyes.

"Can I bring my dad?"

Author's face lit up. "Now you're cooking with gas, Toby!"

Cooking with gas? What does that even mean?

"That's a great idea! A brilliant idea! Why didn't I think of that!" Author jotted a note in his notebook.

Toby threw back his Avengers bedspread and moved to get out of bed. "Boy, will Dad be surprised!"

But Author put his hand up.

"Not so fast, Toby. We need to let things play out a bit in *RiverHome* first in order to set up the next adventure."

"Play out like how?"

"We don't know yet, do we? That's why it's called a cliffhanger." Author scribbled another note.

"When?" Toby asked with a yawn.

"When what?"

"When can we go back?" Toby yawned again.

"Soon," Author replied.

Toby could sense his eyes begging for sleep. He slowly lied down... *or is it laid down... Whatever!* Toby put his head on his pillow.

As he felt himself drifting off a question snuck into his mind, metaphorically speaking.

"Are you the one who put those weird sayings and thoughts into my head, like *worked a charm* and *hominess* and *homonym* and *stepping into a pun*?"

Indubitably!

"Indubitawhat?" Toby barely made out the word above Author's head before his eyes closed.

And with that, Author said as he jotted in his notebook, **Toby Baxter fell asleep. Sad in a way. Indubitably is such a good word!**

The End

Want more Toby Baxter? Sign up at www.TimWrightbooks.com for the *free* Prequel: ***I.C.E. call Toby Baxter*** and a *free* PDF for parents on the power of adventure stories for kids, *and* to be the first to know when Toby launches his next adventure: *RiverHome for the Holidays*. (See the excerpt below.)

The Adventures of Toby Baxter
Book 2:
RiverHome for the Holidays (Excerpt)

PROLOGUE

You Better Watch Out...

Toby Baxter stared at the clock on the wall. 30 minutes until Winter Break... 29 minutes and 50 seconds until Winter Break... 29 minutes and 45 seconds left until Winter Break. Each second felt like an eternity.

Mrs Grayson, his English Literature teacher (and his mom's best friend—inconvenient!) was doing her best to remind the class that they would be writing a short story once Winter Break was over. She hoped that everyone would use the break to think about their topic and...

Toby sighed, turned, and looked out the window at the thickening clouds. So far, little snow had fallen in Minneapolis. But fingers crossed the coming storm would dump several feet of it over the next several days.

Months earlier Toby had stared out this same window when he saw Deckor for the first time. From the second story window he couldn't quite tell if Deckor was a boy or a small man. He looked strangely like a hobbit from the J.R.R. Tolkien book. But it turned out that Deckor was a River Elf, from a place called *RiverHome*, accessed through Toby's closet, of all things. Deckor, along with his sister, Clovor, his brother, Phoenix, and his cousins Judah and Mathilda, had called upon Toby to help them take on Clygon and his legion of trolls.

Something in the front of the classroom caught his attention. He looked away from the window back to Mrs Grayson only to discover that Author was leading the class. He sat on the edge of the teacher's desk, a notebook in his large right hand and a pencil in the left. Through his reading glasses he winked at Toby and scribbled something in the notebook.

Toby looked around at the other students. They all seemed frozen in time. He peeked up at the clock and noticed that it had stopped blinking the seconds. Apparently, only Toby could see Author.

Hello, Toby! It's so good to see you again.

The words appeared above Author's head as he spoke them. He could see Toby looking slightly above his head and made another note in the notebook.

Author was a big man with a deep voice. Toby believed him to be quite old, perhaps in his 50's? His oval head was bald. Toby couldn't tell if Author had lost his hair or liked to shave his head. But today his head was covered by a Santa hat. His graying goatee had morphed into what looked like a graying Santa beard. He was wearing boots, jeans, and the ugliest ugly Christmas sweater Toby had ever seen. It was hideous. Christmas green with a snowman, reindeer, a Christmas Tree, Christmas presents, and various kinds of shiny thingies all over it. Although, Toby had to admit, the Christmas green seemed to match Author's eyes.

"Hey, Author. What are you doing here?"

It looks like the words are above my head once again. You know what that means...

"I'm not... into the story... yet? Which means... there's a story coming?"

That depends.

"On what?"

The Prologue.

"What's a Prologue?"

A Prologue introduces a story. It sets the stage for what's about to happen. It introduces the reader to the adventure up ahead by teasing out a few of the themes that will shape the story.

"Um... ok..."

Like... Author thought for a moment. How about Easter Eggs?

"Easter Eggs?"

Apparently, Easter Eggs have become hip and groovy in books and songs and movies.

"Hip? Groovy? When were you born?"

So, putting the phrase, "Easter Eggs" into the Prologue gets the story off and running.

"I'm not sure that's what Easter Eggs means in a song or a..."

Easter Eggs. Check.

Author wrote something in his notebook and smiled. Then he thought some more.

Clygon...

Toby felt a surge of fear at the sound of that name.

"Clygon? What about Clygon?"

Author frowned. He wrote again in the notebook.

The Christmas Giant.

"Trouble."

The words above Author's head had disappeared.

Toby almost leaped—*or is it leapt?*—out of his desk chair. "Is the Christmas Giant in trouble? Does it have something to do with Clygon?"

Author closed his notebook, took off his reading glasses, and put the pencil behind his ear. "I see you are no longer looking above my head, Toby. You are now once again in the story…"

"Toby! Toby Baxter! Earth to Toby!"

Toby looked up to see his teacher, Mrs Grayson, looking at him. He sensed the whole class was staring at him.

"Toby, I know you're excited to start Winter Vacation but before the bell rings, can you summarize for the class what a Prologue is?"

Toby could feel his face turning red. His friend, Sid, flashed him a big, goofy Sid smile.

"A Prologue is an, um, ah, is… a way… to get… a story started. It sets the stage for what's about to happen."

"Excellent, Toby. I was sure you were daydreaming but you proved me wrong once again.

"OK, class, I'm only giving you one small project to do during Winter Break."

The whole class, including Toby, groaned.

"Write up a Prologue for your short story. Remember, your story is due at the end of January. The Prologue doesn't have to be long. But take the time to set up your…"

The bell rang.

"Have a nice vacation," Mrs Grayson shouted. But no one heard her. The class had vanished out the door into the hallway and out into the coming snow storm.

Because there had been little snow so far and the temps were mild, Toby had ridden his bike to school. Now, flying down one street after another to his house, Author's words chased after him: *Clygon. The Christmas Giant. Trouble.*

He quickly parked his bike in the garage and rushed into the house, past his father, who was unsuccessfully trying to bake Christmas cookies, and into his bedroom. He threw his backpack onto his bed and ran into the closet… straight into the back wall.

Hard.

Knocking him onto his back.

That was going to leave a mark.

You can join Toby on his next adventure to RiverHome at www.TimWrightbooks.com.

Made in the USA
Monee, IL
29 September 2024

66435349R00114